WORLD WAR II

BOOK FOUR

THE LIBERATORS

CHRIS LYNCH

SCHOLASTIC INC.

This book, this series, is dedicated to Nick Eliopulos, who taught me what The Buddy System really means.

ISBN 978-0-545-86986-7

10 9 8 7 6 5 4 3 2 1   15 16 17 18 19

Printed in the U.S.A.   23
First printing 2015

Book design by Christopher Stengel

PART ONE
POLLYWOGS

CHAPTER ONE

New Heights

Our first jump is off this bitty little platform, like a swimming pool diving board, only onto turf instead of into water. I jumped off boulders higher than that thing when I was a kid. This is just to practice our landings, so nobody breaks any legs with carrying all the extra weight of the gear and all. Forward rolling, that's the key, forward with a rightward twist, so you half-corkscrew to the ground onto your hip, then flat forward with both arms stretched ahead like you're bodysurfing.

The trick is all in the knees. Landing stiff, trying to tough it out and remain upright, that's a chump's game. Instructor compared it to a contest of smash-up: one very stupid marine vs. planet Earth. Earth was so far undefeated and would likely remain that way for the foreseeable future.

But, guys being guys, and this being the Marine Corps, there are still a number of broken legs. Our course has a forty percent dropout rate, between one thing and another. Heh. Love that statistic. Always will love that statistic. Makes me laugh. Heh.

We soon move up from the platforms to the towers — water towers and suchlike. Anything pretty high that doesn't tend to have pedestrians under it, in harm's way of a bunch of leatherneck lunkheads dropping out of the sky and squashing them. We are the new secret weapons, the marine paratroopers, the paramarines, and if I got a nickel every time I heard the word *elite* used to describe the kind of force we were gonna be, I could pile them nickels up into a jump tower so high none of us would survive it.

The Eastern Shore League had folded up its tent at the end of the 1941 season, like most of the quality minor league operations did. Nobody ever came right out and said so, but I guess it just seemed suddenly really dumb to have the fittest guys in America playin' ballgames when the rest of the world was out there killing each other in a war that was without a doubt gonna eventually include the USA. Of course, guys like me were always gonna join up anyway, but maybe others would have been happier playin' ball and hoping for the best as far as all the fighting and fate-of-the-free-world business was concerned.

So the leagues, especially the quality ones like the

class-D-level ESL where I was playing proudly for the Major League–affiliated Centreville Red Sox, went and made the decision easier for everybody. They did that by suspending operations for the duration of the war. And, as much as I enjoyed my time in Maryland, bashing baseballs and embarrassing pitchers on my way to eventually joining the big club up in Boston, I agreed completely that this was the right thing to do.

And so, the *next* right thing to do was obvious.

"You *know* I have flat feet," my pal Zachary Klecko said to me when I called him up from our hometown of Sandusky, Ohio.

I laughed a lot at that, wasting a good deal of valuable long-distance phone time in the process. He could always make me laugh, that boy, without hardly even trying.

"Sure, I know that," I said eventually. "You were the only guy I ever saw who could absolutely mash a ball off the wall in deep left center and *still* get thrown out at first base by three steps."

It was his turn to burn up valuable long-distance phone time, but with his punishing, faintly growling silent treatment.

Then, "That happened *once*, Nardini, all right? *Once.*"

"Exactly," I said. He was playing right into my

hands like we both knew he would from the moment he picked up the phone. Like he always played into my hands. "Most of the time there was nothing wrong with your feet at all. They're only maybe a *little* bit flat. In every other way, *you* are just the fighting machine your country needs right now. You. Exactly you. Seen the recruiting posters? Some of them actually have your name on them, I swear. *Uncle Sam wants YOU, Mr. Zachary Klecko!* I promise, I saw one of those in the window of the post office on Meigs Street."

That made him sigh, real loud. That's how I knew I had him and the hook was in deep. The surrender sigh of his, it's a sigh with *oomph*, like a pneumatic drill, that's how I always knew.

"I have a really good thing going here in Detroit, Nick. Ford takes good care of its people. And they're building a plant over in Ypsilanti that's just for the purpose of manufacturing bomber aircraft for the war. B-24 Liberators, Nick. I already have a job lined up there, the day the plant opens, so I know I'm doing my part and there's no way you can make me feel otherwise."

The next valuable stretch of silence between us was not an accident and it was well spent.

"Uh-huh," I said, very sympathetically.

"And I got a gal up here. Her name is Rose, and I've

been dying for you to meet her. And Rose got a job, too, up at the Ypsilanti plant, and we're gonna be going together, and building them Liberators, and so, like I said, doing our bit for the war effort . . ."

This time, out of respect because there was a lady involved, I remained silent for just a bit longer, like I was thinking about it, even though it was just for show.

"That's nice," I said. "But, no."

"Um. No?"

"No. Yes, I'm sorry, but it's no. I am sure Miss Rose is lovely and I am sure she will agree with me."

"Ha!" my old pal bellowed over the line. "You haven't even met her yet. But of course you're sure; you're always sure. So what, exactly, is it that my Rose is supposed to agree with you about?"

Oh, that was my boy, reliable as the tides.

"With this," I said. "Rosie and I both know that you, my friend, are not meant to be *building* Liberators. You are meant to *be* one."

I wasn't bothered when he followed several speech-less seconds of breathing by saying, "I'm hanging up on you now." I wasn't even bothered when he made good on that threat.

Because we both knew. And we both knew that we knew.

Of course, I felt guilty. Naturally. I wasn't some heartless, selfish, good-looking beast. There I was, luring probably the greatest guy in the world out of his perfectly respectable and productive civilian life to come out to play with me. Possibly resulting in the grisly death of one or the other of us, but my hunch was both.

But I couldn't help myself. I was no more able to refrain from dragging Klecko on any great big unknown of an adventure than he was to resist me. So we were just being us, is what we were doing.

Right? Right.

Okay, certain things I was known for, and you could ask anybody. Modesty prevents me from saying handsomeness, because a gentleman should leave that to the judgment of others. But the things that I had earned a reputation for — for my whole life, practically — were these: I was a great baseball player, and I would be again if I didn't get killed serving God and country. I love my God and my country and my baseball. I am loyal; I am reliable, tough, willing. I suppose it should also be disclosed in the interest of fairness that there would be some out there, especially in the baseball fraternity, especially in the Eastern Shore League, who might add that I was known for being a bit mouthy.

Though it could also be added that those people saying that were more than a little bit jealous.

Confidence. If there was one word that all those people would tell you was the one word that could maybe sum me up, I suppose that word would be *confidence*. I always liked to show a lot of it. Everybody knew that about me. Confidence, that was Nick Nardini, and everybody knew it within the first three seconds of knowing me.

But then again, maybe mostly nobody knows anybody else. Not really. It's a hard thing to do, actually, to know somebody inside. To know about the confidence he has, and the confidence he possibly doesn't have.

Maybe nobody knows anybody. Or maybe, everybody is allowed one somebody who truly does. One some buddy.

And there are certain things you just can't do without that one some buddy.

"It's not a guarantee, you know," the recruiting sergeant said as Zachary Klecko signed the paperwork that sealed the deal that was, apparently, not a guarantee.

"What?" Klecko said, looking up and looking stunned at the sergeant while I pried the pen out of my old friend's paw in order to sign my own enlistment papers.

"Like I said," the sergeant said, "it's a sort of gentleman's agreement, more than it is a binding commitment. The Corps will, of course, do everything within reason to keep two good buddies together —"

"Right," Klecko cut in, kind of desperately. "The buddy system."

"Yes," the sergeant said calmly. He spoke more calmly, in fact, with each signature he witnessed. "But it is more of an informal system. An aspiration, if you will, more than a pledge to keep two recruits together come what may. Especially in a wartime situation, especially in an unprecedented global conflict such as the one we are witnessing today, there are so many variables, so many different sets of demands and requirements, in so many different countries. And even those demands are constantly changing, adapting to meet the hundreds and hundreds of challenges that, frankly, only the United States Marine Corps could ever meet. Under the circumstances, we could hardly offer guarantees. You understand that, certainly."

He always breathed heavily, whistley, through his nose when he was mad or confused or frustrated, and so now Zachary Klecko was sounding like a bull about to charge, practically pawing at the ground as he tried to form the words.

"I understand that now," he said. "I didn't understand it in the same way *at all* when you laid it all out
before I signed."

I was just about ready to talk my pal down. Then
the smiling, nodding, distracted reaction of the recruiter
made *me* want to punch the guy, as he looked right past
us to the next pair of young simps coming through the
door. "You'll be fine," the sergeant said without bothering to look at us anymore. "You will be together right
through basic training at the very least. I can give you
my word on that. Then, as long as you meet the same
criteria, pass the same tests, match up with the same job
specs and demands along the way . . . I see no reason
why any two buddies should be denied the opportunity
to see out their USMC commitments together, from this
moment on to their date of discharge."

Right to the end, he failed to look at us. He gradually
rose from his seat, offered us a hand to shake across the
Formica top of his gray metal desk, and started his gravi-
tation toward the new pair of guppies he had in his sights.

I found it almost funny, watching the sharky guy at
work, until I felt Klecko leaning hard in the direction of
following after him.

I grabbed my buddy, throwing an arm most firmly
around his thick and stiffened neck.

"You heard the man," I said. "As long as we do it all right, as long as we match up. As long as we want it enough to work at it, they will keep us together. Buddy."

By degrees, he stopped leaning toward the confrontation. He settled into my grip.

"Buddy," he said, looking right into my face. "It's up to us. We'll do this together, the whole way. Together. Right?"

"You and me," I said. "The whole way."

CHAPTER TWO

It's What Buddies Do

At first, the Marine Corps kept their word. Klecko and I were sent through the process shoulder-to-shoulder. Physical exam, smartness exam, every test they had on offer, we were allowed to take them on the same day, to compare notes, make adjustments, and finally, report in for basic training at Parris Island, South Carolina, lock-step, together.

It was from this point on that they would try to separate us. Not that it was a personal thing, like they were singling us out for any special attention out of spite or anything. It was just that the tests got, out of necessity, increasingly difficult and increasingly specialized, designed to draw each man's strengths and skills out to the point where they could be best utilized by the Corps. Which meant, of course, that they were working out how each man could best serve his country in this pitched battle of good vs. evil.

I laughed out loud the first time I heard a test commandant say that, just 'cause it sounded like it came out of a Superman comic. Commandant didn't laugh, but he did make a point of asking me my name again and writing it down for later, when I'm sure he knocked points off my test score. Apparently, people could do things like that on this new team I was joining, where everybody had a rank and I was at the bottom looking up. I quickly learned to keep that kind of laughter to myself.

The important thing about basic training at Parris Island was that they tested a guy physically and mentally before sending him off to war. If you could take Parris from these drill instructors, the saying went, then you could take Paris from the Nazis. I heard that said four different times before somebody wrote it down and I finally understood what they were all talking about. Not the Nazis, who I was pretty clear on. But the Paris thing. One of them has an extra R, but you can't hear it. Doesn't make a guy stupid.

Me and Klecko, we were prepared. Even with his semi-flat feet, he was capable of whatever challenge was set for him. As I knew he would be. I didn't care how flat his feet were or how many too-many-seconds it took him to run a hundred yards, or how easy it was to enrage him to tears with a simple "your mother" or "your sister" joke. He was the very man. The one I wanted fighting by my side, or, okay, maybe a couple strides behind my side. The one I knew I could count on. The one who would make me braver and tougher than I really was, and would always somehow make up those couple of strides to *be there* when I needed him.

In fact, he showed up at basic training already in better shape than I'd ever seen before, better than in his baseball days, high school, any of it. He'd always been a big guy, but now he was broader, harder. I suspected he'd even somehow gotten faster, which wasn't supposed to happen after a certain age, I didn't think.

So, of course, we made it through the seven weeks of basic together. That was almost easy. Because first, we were honest athletes from way back, so that part was never going to be a problem. And we were no dummies, neither of us, most of the time. So we matched up fairly well right along the line, no reason for anybody to break their word and split us up. And if my time in the fifty-yard dash suddenly and mysteriously got a few seconds slower, I had no worry about my speed coming right back when I needed it to beat out an infield single.

We were about to graduate from being mere boots to being marines, and we were anticipating where in this whole crazy mess of a war we were going to be assigned, together, when a posting appeared. We were just out of the showers, pulling on fresh, clean gear after scraping one more day's sweat and Carolina clay off us. A couple of still-grimy guys filed past us in the other direction at the same time I saw the flier stuck to the board.

To be honest, I was swallowing a whole lot of worrying over that *together* part of what was to come. I couldn't think of how we were going to ensure it, until I clapped eyes on this.

Special Marine Corps personnel sought. Must be equal to highest demands of fitness, ingenuity, creativity, and heretofore unforeseen individual challenge. Candidates must possess flexibility of mind and body, openness to new modes of military concept, and must be unmarried. Danger and uncertainty, as well as adventure, of this new undertaking must be stressed.

Ideal candidates can look forward to a further intensified period of maximum physical and mental testing and training, successful completion of which will result in a substantial boost in both monthly pay and daily challenge. If all of the above sounds like it appeals to you, then please contact your Senior Drill Instructor.

"Are you thinking what I'm thinking?" I said as I read the posting, with Klecko's moist dog breath huffing right into my ear.

"Y'know, Nicky," he said, still huffing, "I wasn't even thinking yet about what *I* was thinking at all. I was thinking about what *you* were thinking. Because whatever *you're* thinking somehow always seems to matter a lot more to my life than what *I'm* thinking. And I was thinking that you were thinking that we both should be thinking about going for this thing."

I turned, so that my ear was no longer in his face, but my eyes were right up at his eyes.

"We'll be great at this," I said.

"They'll never let me in," he said. "Not in a million years. Not with my flat feet, not with my slowness. This time, buddy, you're going to have to go on without me. But you should."

Bless him, Klecko was no actor. He was so gamely unconvincing you'd think I just suggested shooting his puppy because it had fleas. But he went on talking. "It'll be perfect for you, so you should go. I want you to go. The buddy system . . . ah, that was always just kid stuff anyway, right? This is something else. You should do it. This buddy hereby releases you —"

"So, you agree," I said. "We'll be great at this."

"When did you hear that? I never agreed nothin' with you. And then there's Rose. We were talking about getting married. First chance I got for an extended leave, we were gonna do it. And you saw, no marrieds need apply."

"Yeah," I said, "you're right. We will be great at this."

"Uh-huh, Nick, you just go ahead; go right on hearing stuff that nobody said and the only Special Marine Unit you're gonna see is the kind of unit where they strap you down on your bed for your own safety."

"Ahhh," I said then, turning on him with a crazy wide grin and crazier wide arms like I was about to give him one of those big hugs of mine that he always said he never wanted. I knew better, though.

"Stop it, you," the big bruiser said, backing away from me, like a bear afraid of a squirrel.

So I did, I stopped advancing just like he told me to. And he stopped retreating. He didn't stop eying me suspiciously, though.

"You're still grinning at me kind of nutty, Nicky, and like you know something I don't know and probably don't want to know."

I had to laugh. The guy could just always somehow make me laugh at any situation.

"No," he said firmly. "I know what you're thinking and the answer is no, so don't even waste your breath saying it. The regular Marines is going to be hard enough and dangerous enough without us needing to go join some extra crazy daredevil version that they're apparently just now making up, out of nowhere."

"It's not out of nowhere; it's from the top guys, it's all over the announcement. You can just about smell the danger and thrill right off the poster. You wanna know where nowhere is, that's Ypsilanti, Michigan. *That*, my dear Klecko, is nowhere. Which, by the way, I rescued you from and am still patiently awaiting my thank-you for."

Now I'd gone and done it. I'd turned the bear back into a bear, and I had to shake my furry tail quick to squirrel out of range of his lunge.

"*Rescued?*" He growled as convincingly as any bear I'd ever meet. "Nardini, you kidnapped me. Right out of a whole complete life that I had with a great job and the best girl and everything. *You* are the only reason I am this far into the danger zone, and now you wanna talk me into going further?"

He hadn't said one untrue or unfair thing. He never did, ever, as a matter of fact. There was no decent response to his argument.

He huff-chuff-sighed, like a steam locomotive pulling into a station.

"Why, Nicky? Tell me that, huh? *Why?*"

"Because, Zacky, you know just as well as I do that you and me always did this. Exactly this. Remember? If there was a higher, a tougher, a bigger, a further —"

"A morer," he said solemnly.

"Of course, you remember. All-out, every time, that was us."

"Until the day I couldn't cut it anymore, Nick."

"That was us," I say, talking over him. "And now it's gonna be us again. Whatever special force the Marines have in mind, we already know they mean us. *We* are a special force already, you and me. They are in for the fight and so are we. And if you're in a fight . . . well, I don't gotta tell you."

"When you're in a fight you take it to 'em, you don't wait on them."

"And, when you're in a fight . . . ?"

"You don't stop, until there is no fight."

"Buddy, I think you just defined the United States Marine Corps."

There was an odd, funny minute of silence between us then, and for once I couldn't read my old pal so clearly.

"I didn't mean that," he finally said in a gravelly sort of whisper.

"What? Didn't mean what?"

"The whole kidnapping bit. It's not like that."

"Ah, yeah, Kleck, I know. I mean, for one thing, look at the size of you."

"Ha," he said, still seeming too serious a fellow to convince me otherwise with any kind of half laugh. "Listen, I gotta go over to the rec hall. Feel like I need to punch the heavy bag for a little while."

"Sure," I said, "that sounds like a good idea."

Without saying anything more he did a quick and militarily sound heel-pivot and marched briskly out the exit.

It was about fifteen seconds later when he presented his big cranium just inside the halfway-opened door. "Aren't you coming?" he asked, sounding almost like he'd gotten lost. "Who's supposed to hold the bag for me otherwise? I thought you enjoyed holding the bag for me."

He certainly seemed to believe he was involved in some kind of debate or other.

"I do," I said, following him out the doorway.

It was a quick walk to the rec hall, and I let him set the pace. He was rolling out his patented Klecko silent treatment, eyes forward and mouth shut, but I could sense the sourness of his mood begin to lift. We were, after all, closer to his comfort zone with every step we took toward punching stuff.

The silence, though.

Silence was maybe my least favorite thing in the world. Give me noise any day. Any minute of every day. I expected to encounter a lot of horrifying things once I got to the war. But I was still betting that when I came out again, silence was going to remain right up there at the top of the list of unbearables.

This, of course, was well known to my best friend, who was giving me a whole bath in the silence stuff.

"So it's a yes, then?" I blurted, just a bit too loud to not sound nutty, once we'd stepped into the rec hall.

He stopped short, and as he did, my nose left its impression in the back of his khaki green T-shirt. Then he rammed a bam of his elbow into my ribs, just to put a bit of distance between us.

He was already popping lightly at the bag by the time I made my wounded, winded, hunched-over way to him.

More silence. I didn't like it.

And then the lug spoke.

"You know my answer, Nicky. It's the same answer as last time, and the time before that, and so on all the way back."

He spoke real soft, but he made well sure that at least the bag got his message emphatically.

It hurt my ribs to laugh, but I laughed. It hurt my ribs to hold the bag while he savaged it, but I held the bag.

The buddy system. Who said it wasn't a real thing, huh?

CHAPTER THREE

Higher and Higher

I don't know why I ever even doubted it. He almost had me convinced on the flat feet problem. But of course they welcomed Klecko and me with open arms into the Marine Parachute Battalion specialist training program. We were as fit and ready as anybody — which, as it turns out, wasn't entirely fit or entirely ready. Because basic training at Parris Island hadn't, in reality, gotten us into the superb physical condition we had thought.

What basic had done was get us into condition to *get* into condition. Paramarine-style condition.

Camp Lejeune, North Carolina, is where we go to jump school. Over sixteen further-intensified weeks of training, we do in fact learn to jump. And to run. And to climb and to fall and to navigate and to starve and to broil and to sweat such a sweat that I cannot believe it is coming out of my own pores. I could swear it is actual, honest-to-goodness USMC green, the stuff that oozes out of me. They push us so hard to see what we are capable of physically — and find out where our weaknesses might be psychologically — I am sure that if this were anywhere else but the Corps, then much of it would be illegal. Maybe it is anyway.

I do all right. Never end one day with an ounce of anything left in my tank, but also never fail to answer the call to roll out of the sack in the morning and take on whatever new challenge they want to throw at us.

It changes a guy, no question about it. The Marines know what they're doing, especially the special services training like this. It might look like they're just in it to see if they can kill a guy within the allotted sixteen weeks that they get a shot at him. But of course it's not that way at all. It's exactly the opposite. They want to make the guy unkillable. And make him a killer elite while they're at it.

And I wouldn't guess they've ever done this with greater success than they have with Zachary Klecko of Sandusky, Ohio.

"How is this possible?" I ask, breathless from both shock and exertion as I reach the top of the jump tower. It's one of the instructor's favorite conditioning skill drills, having guys race two at a time up to the platform — not to jump, but to race back down again. Klecko has gotten to the top a good five seconds before me.

"I don't know," he says evenly, without even offering a little courtesy wheeze to spare my feelings. "But it's about to happen again."

The instructor's whistle shreds the air, signaling the start of the race to the bottom.

It can be more dangerous going down than going up. They have stressed this to us more than once and insisted how much more careful we need to take it on the down run if we don't want to wind up broken leathernecks.

I must still be twenty feet from the finish when I start hearing my good buddy's distinctive crunchy-snorty chuckle, the one that sounds like he's trying to force dry saltine crackers out through his nose. "That's right," he adds for extra encouragement, "you be good and careful there, now."

I approach him where he's standing next to the instructor, who's slapping him on the back and nodding, just a dog biscuit and a scratch behind the ear short of the full "good boy" treatment. Behind them another dozen guys are lined up waiting for their turn to go head-to-head in the same drill. I try to suppress my heavy breathing, and show Klecko upturned palms meant to be interpreted as *What's so funny?*

I finally ask him, raspy but dignified, "Did I miss something?"

Klecko checks his watch with this big, sweeping gesture, rotating his arm like the reverse windup motion of the biggest jerk pitchers in the Eastern Shore League.

"Yeah, lunch, I think," he says, to the tremendous appreciation of twelve jumping green jerks of the USMC, all of 'em laughing, clapping.

It so happens that I did not miss lunch, and everyone knows it, because we were all told beforehand that we could head straight over for chow once we were done with our drill. Klecko certainly knows it, and he's still grinning away as he lays his muscley arm across my shoulders and leads me in the direction of the mess hall.

"That was fun, eh, Nick?" he says, meaning every bit of it without managing to cover himself in fink at the same time. Probably another gift nobody has but him.

"Fun?" I say like I am distracted by something else, though nothing else interests me at all just now. "Oh, I guess I didn't notice the fun part."

"Ah, don't be such a drip. C'mon, you played for the Centreville Red Sox, for cryin' out loud. You played in front of crowds; people knew your name and screamed when you belted one out of the park or gunned somebody down at the plate with a perfect strike from the deepest part of the outfield . . ."

"Well, I do have a good arm. Not a lot of left fielders —"

"Right. And that, Nick, was the first time anybody's clapped for me. Since high school at least. And even that time it was —"

"For when you got thrown out at first after bashing a ball off the wall."

I put my arm up and around his big dumb shoulders, too.

"Yeah," he says. "Y'know, I'm doing pretty good here, a lot better than I did when we were playing ball together. I'm getting along great, with mostly a great bunch of guys. And I'm starting to feel it, y'know, Nick, about getting into this thing, getting into action and fighting whoever has it coming to 'em, y'know? And I'm ready. I'm so ready . . ."

"Yeah, what is that? No offense, I knew you'd find a way to be good at whatever we had to do, but I wasn't expecting you to turn into the star of the Marine paratroop program. How did all this happen? I mean, you didn't even used to do so good with heights, now all of a sudden you turn into one of the great apes."

"Love," he says, happily, seriously.

"Love," I repeat as we push through the swinging double doors into the noisy mess. "Love made you bigger, stronger, faster, leaner, fearless . . ."

"Yup," he says, without raising his voice, but still managing to make himself heard effortlessly over the hundred chattering, clattering marines eating with their mouths open and their tin utensils beating out no rhythm at all. "Love, and a year in the Civilian Conservation Corps. Built camps up in the mountains, planted thousands of trees. They made me a lumberjack, man, how do you like that. Me, way up in these trees sawing away, making the forests all right. Thank you, CCC, is all I got to say. Did I never tell you about that, Nicky?"

"Ah, no, Zack, I don't think you did."

"Oh, right, y'know, that might have been your bigshot year. Remember, first year of pro ball, thought you were the golden boy and you were kind of a rat. I think that was the year, and you weren't in touch at all and that's how you didn't get told."

"Zack? You were up a *tree*. How was I supposed to be in contact?"

We are at the halfway point in the line and I can see him, the big baboon. He's playing with me now, acting like I'm way down on his list of interests, somewhere the other side of the succotash and Spam they seem to be slinging at us today.

"You didn't know I was up a tree," he says wearily. "And my ma said there were no calls or letters from you."

I am fast running out of dark corners to hide my guilt.

"Ah, your ma. How's she doin', Zack?"

"She's great. She was askin' about you. Askin' if you were still a bighead stuck-up rat and all that."

"Your ma never said that about me."

"She's too polite. She was thinking it, though. I know her very well."

This, apparently, is a thing with him, a real thing that bothers him, that I had not even noticed — which automatically means that I'm guilty. I am about to try to redeem myself — how, I don't know — when he cuts me off just before getting to the head of the line.

"I want to thank you, Nick. For bringing me here. You did me a big favor."

That big looping curveball catches me looking. He gets served his slop just like that, what with there being no choices to make and all. I get slopped in right behind him and we find a couple seats opposite each other at the end of a long table.

"You're welcome," I say. "Bet your ma doesn't feel that way about it, though, am I right?"

"Oh yeah, you're right about that one. And she wasn't even polite about it."

"And we're not even killed yet."

"What did I say about that, Nicky? I mean it." He manages to sound both helpless and menacing.

"All right, all right, I won't talk about our deaths anymore. And I'll steer clear of your ma for a while, huh?"

"Two years, minimum. Oh, and Rosie, too. Turns out you were way off there. She did not agree with you about this, and said if she saw you now she'd pop a line of rivets straight across your forehead. I've seen her work that rivet gun, too, Nick."

"Starting to sound like I'll be safer overseas."

The final week is almost overwhelming, all kinds of sensations weaving in and out of each other and binding up to make every bit of it that much stronger. The physical challenges, forced marches, nearly vertical terrain grappling with no equipment but a pair of marine boots and a pair of marine hands to get the job done. That forty percent figure that was estimated based on US Army paratroop training and the one battalion of para-marines who went through just ahead of us was no joke and it was no boast. Seems to me like it might even have been an underestimate.

So we have a lot more elbow room as we near the finish than we had at the start. Mental exhaustion is catching up on physical exhaustion and you can see it on faces everywhere. There is the anxiety around what is to come next, and then one more completely unex-pected twist.

"Are you gonna miss it here?" Klecko says to me as we line up for the final physical test before the last jump.

"Yeah?" I say, surprised to hear it myself. It's one of those questions you would never think about, for sure never ask yourself, unless somebody brought it up. Or unless you were a guy like Klecko. (So, if you were Klecko. Since there's nobody like Klecko.)

"We're with a lot of good men here, Nick," he says.

"We are," I say. "Which is a good thing, because wherever we're going, we're all going together. Second Marine Parachute Battalion."

"Yeah, good thing, then. I guess all the jerks washed out with the forty percent."

"That'd be my guess."

The diabolically piercing whistle, which I am not going to miss very much, calls us to the line for the start of the drill. The instructor reels off the names of the pairs and the running order for each of them to take on the "bring 'em back alive" challenge. It's a timed obstacle course, modified for a lot more marching up steep inclines and negotiating barbed wire and booby traps than you'd normally see in one of these things. On the bright side, there is less climbing involved, and less sprinting.

Only fair, since you have to do the whole thing with your buddy draped over your shoulder in a fireman's carry the whole way. And then you switch places, and your buddy has to carry you.

I would not say I'm looking forward to this one. I would say I'm the only person in the whole camp who isn't looking forward to it.

Not looking forward to *my* turn at it, that is. There are even bets going around, having nothing to do with my estimated time, but with whether I will die, or faint, or break a bone. Betting was so hot on my nose turning out to be the money bone — when I inevitably fell on my face with a full Klecko pack on my back — that they had to take it off the board. My spine then became quite popular.

Six pairs across the whole camp have been selected for the field, which is an honor in itself for sure. Of the six, the team of Klecko and Nardini is slotted . . . well, now. Sixth. It is a kind of honor. It certainly isn't due to random names out of a hat. The show needs a big finale, and if not superb athletic accomplishment, then a train wreck will do.

Zack has his arm draped hard over my shoulders as the first pairing goes off. He really squeezes, as if he thinks I might try and take a powder before I'm mashed into one. It's a warm and brotherly kind of embrace, in the midst of the crowd of cheering, hollering paramarines who are about to ship off to someplace nasty, together, like a giant family of skyjumping lunatics. But even through the excitement and the roaring and the fraternity of the moment, I can feel the rumble of Klecko's laughter through his rib cage. Then, another jump school joker walks up and makes the gimme-gimme motion with his hand at Klecko. Money is exchanged, laughter is shared, and the guy moves on.

I shove Zack away from me, pointing at his happy, sneaky mug.

"You!" I bark. "You placed a bet? You . . . bet I would . . . *what*, man? What could you even . . . ?"

"Nicky, man, it's all in fun. It don't mean nothin'."

"What? What happened to loyalties? The buddy system?"

I am accomplishing nothing more than making him laugh harder with every word I say.

"The buddy system still holds, Nick, no matter what. That comes first. But, you could really help me out here. If you do find yourself going down, try and land on your left forearm. That's all I'm saying. Think left. Think forearm."

It isn't often in my life that a situation has left me speechless. Possibly never, in fact. And I'm not going to let this be the first.

"Yeah," I say, "well maybe I'll just land on my neck and snap it, just to make sure you lose your money. Who'll be laughing then?"

It is, in reality, my first attempt to contribute a joke to the whole foolishness. Turns out it is the first thing that manages to bleed the laughter out of my pal altogether.

"Don't do that," he says, gripping me bone-crushingly hard with one paw on each of my shoulders. He brings his face up close and hard enough to mine that for an instant I brace for the granddaddy of all headbutts. Though I would never expect him to do that in a million years, I am royally pleased when he doesn't.

"Okay," I say, trying to match his grimness. "I won't do that."

We turn our attention then, like everybody else, to the remarkable men busting their guts out over that brutal course. Klecko joins the roaring cheer as the third pair finish, staggering and tumbling across the finish line like a circus act.

I know, like Zack knows, like we all know, as we cheer. That the whole bunch of us will be busting our guts out very shortly. It will be someplace at least an ocean away, and it will be for keeps.

So I remind myself to knock it off with teasing Zachary Klecko or anybody else about broken necks and grisly deaths.

When the time finally comes for couple number six to step up and give the people what they came for, the noise goes strangely down, almost subdued. Maybe there's real money on the line. Maybe there's genuine concern for my well-being all of a sudden. Maybe I should have thought of this before, but could be a lot of folks are really here to see my buddy put in an effort for the ages.

Because he just well could.

"What are you doing?" I say, when he makes as if he

is going to be the one carried on the fireman's shoulder for the first leg.

"Let's just get it out of the way, Nick. Everybody's had their fun. Just take it slow and even, let your legs do everything, don't mess up your back. Cruise, is all. If we lose a couple seconds to the other guys, I'll have a chance to try and make 'em back up for us."

"No."

"No? Why?"

"Because everybody came hoping to see me as the last act, and they shouldn't be disappointed."

"Ah, now —"

"And," I say, retaking my rightful place as the senior member of this firm, "I'm planning on you laying down a fast time, so I can beat it."

He's been bent half over like a marionette with its strings cut. But for this, he stands to attention.

"Yeah?" he says, beaming.

"Yeah," I say, beaming, or wincing — somewhere in that range.

"Let's show these boys how buddies get the job done, then," he says, and my response is sliced away by the vicious whistle. I jump up, go limp, and Klecko is already making tracks when he catches me on his shoulder, turns, and starts chewing that turf up like a racehorse.

The crowd noise goes back up to the level of a roar, and I am in a unique position to take it all in as my stallion thunders over the first thirty yards of flat terrain. My whole body bucks and bounces while Klecko proves that it can be done, running this test and not just marching it. I cannot believe it myself at first, but when I look down at his feet he is managing it by doing that same old horsey-skip we all did as kids, pretending to be cowboys on wild mustangs in the schoolyard.

Then I look at the crowd again, the guys. The noise is rowdy and it is real. Better than that, though, is the spirit of it.

Baseball — the Eastern Shore League in particular — has taught me the difference between a crowd that is behind you and one that is not. Some towns with great baseball fans will clap for a nifty catch or a sharp stolen base even if it's not the home team pulling it off. There are others, lots, that don't feel that way at all. Like the fans of the rancid Federalsburg A's, who, I am convinced, have all contracted rabies. That's how they all act toward you: like rabid dogs. Unless you play for the A's — and frankly, I'd rather have rabies.

Point being, I know a crowd that shouts to beat you down from one that makes the biggest racket just to push you to show them what your best is. As I bumble along, backward and tilted sideways, from this big gang of loons, I know I'm not playing in front of the Federalsburg A's crowd, is how I would put it.

"So, how much would you say I weigh?" I ask, because what else do you do in a spot like this?

"One seventy," he says immediately. "Definitely not more than one seventy-three."

"Ah, precise. And you?"

"Two hundred and twelve."

"Not a great ratio, really."

"Nick, I think you should probably save your breath, since you'll need it later. For breathing."

"Yeah, right. Okay."

That would be the difference between my guy and a thoroughbred. They would have a lot in common, but the racehorse wouldn't be calming the jockey down, or calling out "Duck!" as we approach a wire crossbar, or "Hop!" just before we clear the small, but deep, water hazard.

As we approach the end of the course and all our peers cheer wildly for the new all-time record setter, I could not be more proud. Almost too proud to be worried about what's coming next.

He promises to talk me through every inch. Unfortunately, it's the pounds, not the inches, that take me three mighty heaves to get the load balanced. "If you tell me it's all in the legs, by the way, I'm going to dump you on your head."

"I was gonna say it's all in the head, but I don't want to know what you'll say about that."

"That's right," I groan. "You don't."

When I want to fall, Zack says he won't allow it. When I want to surrender with dignity, just put him on his feet and let us walk together for the final forty yards, he growls in my ear, "Aren't you better than this? The line is *right there*. If you quit on this, where else are you gonna quit?"

My buddy is so infuriating, so full of authority in spite of hanging over my shoulder and basically speaking directly into my butt, that he all but drowns out any other sound.

But eventually I hear it. The crowd, the guys. As I stagger down the stretch, not likely to break the record held by the guy I'm carrying, I start to hear the cheering. It is huge, like a wall or a wave of sound about to break right over us.

And I realize it's for me, for us, and I wish I didn't, because it's making me all sappy, all dopey emotional, just at the point where more people are looking at me, focused on just me, at the same time than ever before in my life.

It also makes me stronger. Between that wave of noise in front and Klecko's threats behind me, I get a new surge of energy and speed that picks me up, picks both of us up, and practically hurls us weightless over those last yards and over the finish line at some speed.

My time is last, by a lot. I am mobbed at the finish just the same, by my pals, my comrades, and my buddy.

I didn't break any records. But I didn't break any bones, either.

We have come a long way during this adventure already. We are changed. The world is changed. People are slapping my back because Zachary Klecko is my friend, and who doesn't love Zachary Klecko? After all this time, I've suddenly become his sidekick.

War, it upends everything. And we aren't even in it yet.

"I think I'm getting sprinkled with some of your stardust," I say to my partner as we soak it all up.

"Ah, I figured it was time," he says.

My goodness, but the Marines have already done so much for this man.

We have jumped. Off of barrels, low rooftops, high treetops, and water towers. We jumped off a tower at the base in Lakehurst, New Jersey, that they said was built for the World's Fair. We jumped onto beaches, into valleys, and over mountains. We jumped from a blimp, and we jumped at night into total blackness and faith.

Now is it. The Show. We approach the drop zone, a fairly easy broad swath of green grass that will be devoured by cows tomorrow but is ours for right now. We are in our borrowed Army troop transport plane, which makes the occasion special enough, because it is already clear to us that the Army does not want to share or help us out in any way.

But this is our graduation exam, after all.

The fat tube of the body of the plane is lined on each side by a long bench, each of which is right now supporting a half dozen raw marine butts. There is a cable attached to a track that runs along the ceiling between the two rows of guys. When the call comes, we will stand up in line and each clip our pull cords to that rip wire. That way, when we jump, the rip wire will yank the cord, releasing our chutes, so we don't have to even think. It's always good when we don't have to think.

"Now!" the jump leader calls, and I get to my feet. I am number one in line, with Klecko right behind me. I stand at the edge of the hatch, wide-open to the elements and the land hundreds of feet below us. Just wide-open to it all.

I reach back just after hooking on, and I bump him in the ribs with the side of my hand. He does something like the same to my back.

"Go!" the man calls, and without hesitation, I do.

There is nothing like it. The sensation — watching the world come up, foot by foot, to greet me — is untouchable. The world, on every horizon, is for me; it is all there for me. The green below, the blue-white above. The violent wind trying to blow me backward, to stuff me back into that plane, is thrilling beyond words. But it is not going to win. I am never going back no matter how hard it blows.

I've known ever since I was a kid that flying was going to be everything, and it was going to be better than all other possibilities except for baseball.

I am flying now, descending to an earth I am going to defend from every rotten threat that is trying to ruin her. My best buddy, the best guy in the world, is floating down to the same fate just ten seconds behind me. We can do this. We will not fail, come what may.

I come down too fast and bang hard into the earth, ending the flight that was, if I'm honest, even a little better than baseball. But I land on bent knees, drop corkscrew to my right hip in the tall green grass, and don't feel a thing. As I start reeling in my lines before the wind can catch my chute and drag me halfway to Japan, my buddy drops softly to the same grass forty or so yards away. He bends, twists, rolls, and springs back up. Textbook paramarine.

As we haul in our lines, we look across the field toward each other. Hard to make out faces from that distance, but we know.

We both very much know — we have earned our wings and a whole lot more along the way.

What we do not know is where we are headed.

We don't know as we stand on the parade ground for the ceremony to have our wings pinned on our chests.

We still don't know as we ride the troop train cross-country all the way to San Diego and then board the troop ship that is going to take us to the war.

Obviously we are headed for the Pacific Theater — that much we have known for weeks. But as we steam away from the San Diego naval base, there is still no official word as to the next stop for the six hundred and fifty men of our newly minted Second Marine Parachute Battalion.

The oceangoing segment of the trip is to take eleven days. That's a lot of time for calisthenics, lifeboat drills, arm wrestling contests, and card games, especially for a highly trained, highly excitable population of young marines floating toward a war zone. Hanging out over the edge of the top-deck rail and speculating eventually becomes the activity that consumes most of the guys' time. That is certainly the case for Klecko and me.

Because we are exceptionally clever leathernecks, we have come to a conclusion by around day six. It's the same conclusion that the scuttlebutt around the ship has been putting out there for days already, but a guy shouldn't just take scuttlebutt as fact necessarily unless he wants to wind up looking like a total rube from time to time.

"Guadalcanal," I say to Klecko, as we step out onto the deck to start walking our routine post-breakfast laps around the perimeter of the ship.

"I'm out of any other guesses," he says. "It's the only thing that makes sense."

The First Parachute Battalion has been there for two months already. Which is why we had first ruled it out. But as reports keep coming back about what a rotten slugfest Guadalcanal has become, with a lot of the eleven thousand marines of the initial landing going down killed in action or injured, it starts making more sense. Maybe it should have been our first guess all along, but what do we know about strategy, planning, troop deployment? We know guns, and what to do with them. We know, specifically, machine guns, as our assignments have made official. Because of a few points' difference in our performances on the firing range, I'm rated as Sharpshooter, but Klecko scored in the class above me, which is Expert.

And so we were designated a light machine gun firing team, Klecko as gunner and me as assistant gunner, as part of a ten-man squad within the Demolition Platoon. We are a team, within a team, within a team. Actually, I could carry that further on up and include several more teams that were within other teams that were within other teams.

But however high up the chain you go, it still works its way down to the perfect two-man unit, the buddy system functioning just the way it should. Even if there is the minor hitch that maybe the order of ranking within our perfect two-man unit is not quite what I had figured on.

Our second lap around the deck is disrupted when we're stopped by a group of the more seasoned Navy guys who are permanent crew of the ship. They block our way, then silently hand over papers, one to each of us.

Subpoena and Summons
To Appear Before The Trusty Shellbacks
Of The Court of King Neptune
For Hearing, Verdict, and Sentencing
Pertaining to Gross Violations
of Conduct, Comportment, and
Presentation Policies while Aboard This Vessel

It looks official to me. The presenting party is a uniformly scowling bunch. They certainly appear serious enough. I look to Klecko, who is either still the sadly slow reader he was in high school or is going over it again out of disbelief. His frozen grimace suggests the latter.

"Can I ask what this is about?" I say, as nervous as I have been at any time since joining up.

"You may not," one scowling sailor says.

"It doesn't even say when the hearing is," Klecko says, as he scans worriedly through the document yet again.

I look back at the guy who'd said I couldn't ask.

"So when is it?" I say. I am getting just about irritated enough not to care what might happen if I have to take it up a notch.

The sailor calmly checks his watch. Then he looks up to the ship's control tower, so I do, too. All I notice are the flags and radio locators whipping madly as the winds kick up under quickly darkening skies.

He looks back at his watch. I look at him looking at his watch.

"Y'know," I snap, "this is getting just about —"

"Three, two, one," he says right over me. Then he looks up, grinning. "Now."

"Now?" Klecko spouts.

Then we hear no words at all as the ship's horns blast a long, massive howl across the surface of the ocean that rides the wind and can probably be heard in Japan.

When it's done, the sailor and his henchmen part to wave us through.

"Come, pollywogs, and take your sentence with good grace and cheer," he says, ushering us out to the bow of the ship.

"What kind of a *sentence* ever brought anybody good cheer?" Klecko says to me in a desperate whisper.

"Don't worry, buddy," I say with a loud slap of his broad back that somewhere in my mind functions as a kind of warning to the sailors behind us. "We'll weather it, whatever it is."

And weather it is just what we do. One hour later we are still out on the bow of the ship, in the midst of a driving, squally storm. We are mopping the deck, which — though a crazy thing to be doing at this moment in this weather — is not the crazy part. In fact, we are doing it topless, with bright green dyed hair and in tight-fitting, green sequined skirts that taper all the way down over our feet, which now resemble fins. It is tough to move in these things. Klecko falls twice trying to get around with his mop.

We are mermaids, of course.

The horn blast had signaled the moment when we crossed the equator, entering the Southern Hemisphere. There is a long naval tradition that there needs to be a "ceremony" marking the passage for every first-timer. Every "pollywog," who then graduates from that imma-ture, unformed, and uninitiated form of life.

When we are finally allowed to come inside and

waddle our way belowdecks, soaked to the flippers and shaking, we go straight to our quarters. It takes us an excruciating amount of time to make the relatively short, miserable journey, since we are bound to remain in "uniform" until we can get to the privacy of quarters. If we were seen changing by any unlucky seaman, thus destroying the precious mystery of the mermaid forever, there would be another Subpoena and Summons. And surely nobody wants that.

When we've finally inched our way all the way back, Klecko and I are uncommonly gratified to see the place that has been our bedroom for the past week. As we are about to descale, we find one more surprise. On each of our racks is a personalized certificate, intricate and momentous like a real university degree. It denotes our graduation, our crossing a symbolic line in addition to the geographical one. From no place to someplace.

From the pollywogs we were to the shellbacks we've become.

In its way, it feels as significant to me as my Sharpshooter medal and my wings.

"I didn't know anything about this tradition, did you?" Klecko says, trying to wriggle out of his outfit while admiring his certificate at the same time.

"No. But that's because we were not a part of that tradition. Until now." I wave my paper proudly in the air.

"Y'know, fellas, that's really swell," comes a voice snapping from one of the lower racks. "But could you shut up now so the rest of us can get some shut-eye?"

The rest of them. I look around to see the bunch of guys, brave and certified marine paratroopers, all with green hair and several with mermaid tails still attached as they huddle under their blankets trying to get back to human blood temperature.

PART TWO
SHELLBACKS

CHAPTER FOUR

Uncaged

We don't go to Guadalcanal after all.

We go to New Zealand, for another two months of training. Then we're moved to Camp Kiser, New Caledonia, for a further *nine* months of training.

We're trained now. We are trained beyond belief. Every man in the battalion has by now mastered every weapon in our arsenal. We're to the point where in an emergency situation any one of us could go down and be replaced by somebody else without even being missed.

"I'd miss you anyway, Nardini," Klecko says.

"I appreciate that," I tell him as we step out onto the sunlit deck. "I was just meaning to say that they've got us so finely tuned that I can hardly even think of myself as myself anymore. I think of myself as one component of a much bigger, beautifully designed machine. Like a Cadillac, maybe."

"Or an ant colony," Klecko pipes up.

"Well, or, yeah, I suppose like an ant colony. That works. But don't you feel like that, too? Like you could pick up any weapon on the battlefield and jump right in feeling like an expert?"

"Yeah, sure. I mean, I know twenty-two different horrific ways that I never want to use a Ka-Bar knife, for one thing."

"Right, you don't want to. But you're glad you know how to, for when the time comes, are you not?"

"Absolutely, for when that time comes."

And that time is coming now.

That's probably why we're jabbering the way we are, out of nerves, fear, and adrenaline, and all the banked-up, torqued-up, trained-up *mania* that is finally going to be unleashed on the enemy. Now. Now, now. Now.

We're aboard an LST — that's Landing Ship, Tank — steaming toward the coast of Vella Lavella in the Solomon Islands. As the name suggests, this vessel can carry a bunch of tanks, as many as eighteen, and deposit them right onto a beach if conditions are right. It can also do the same for a whole lot of troops, which it's doing right now. One-third of the Second Parachute Battalion's 650 troopers are on board, along with tons of supplies, ammo, smaller vehicles, and larger artillery. The rest of our troops are spread among several smaller vessels in our convoy. Even from the inside of the big beast, this is a fairly awe-inspiring ship. A few of the guys from my squad and I are just coming out onto top deck, where we hang at the rail along the port side of the bow. Looking that long way down to where our steel hull is crashing through the choppy waters, I can only imagine how terrifying it must look to some unfortunate Japanese infantryman crouched in the bushes when a thing like this breaches like some futuristic mechanical whale and throws itself onto the land right in front of him. When this thing comes crashing into the shore and the giant front ramp drops down to unload all this angry firepower, it'll have to blow the beach defenders into a helpless panic.

I'm certainly hoping so, anyway, and I say as much now.

"Not me, not at all," says JoJo Bryant. He's the other light machine gunner in our squad. The four of us — Klecko and his *assistant*, plus Bryant and his assistant gunner, Bailey Westphal — have become a kind of squad-within-a-squad during our endless and intense months of training.

"Me neither," says Westphal. "We've waited long enough. Time to get ours."

"I gotta agree, Nick," Klecko adds. "We didn't do

all this work just to *scare* the enemy away. I hope they stay right where they are and fight us."

"We'd only have to chase 'em down, anyway, even if they did run," says Bryant. "Because it ain't like they'd be running all that far, going home, giving up. These guys have no intention of quitting, no matter how scary we look."

"Yeah, I know," I say.

And of course I do know. I know what everybody else knows, that the Japanese are fighting our guys all the way to the bloody end. Reports are coming back from across the Pacific that we're getting all we can handle and sometimes more than we can handle. They fight ferociously, craftily, and to the death. We are not to expect many surrenders, under any circumstances.

"And besides," Westphal growls, "we *owe* these boys for everything they've done. And we owe it to our boys to give the vicious little monsters what they got comin' to them."

Now, Westphal is among the most intense and motivated people we've got. He has been itching to sink his choppers into the Japanese for a long time, and if for some reason this mission got canceled at the last minute, I could see him making the trip by himself, swimming all the way if he had to, with his gun in his teeth. But he also pretty well speaks for everybody when he says we owe them. We owe them for Pearl Harbor and the sneakiness of it that still leaves a sharp bitter taste at the back of every American serviceman's throat. We owe them for the relentless way they've marched across the whole region for several years now. They've expanded their empire and swallowed up other nations as if they want to show the Nazis how it's really done.

We'd been hearing about all that in the news and then from our own briefings for long enough that we figured we knew it all.

But then we got to New Caledonia. It was there we joined up with our brothers of the First Parachute Battalion, who had arrived at Camp Kiser straight from being relieved off of Guadalcanal.

And if we'd thought we knew it all, about how the war was going, and about the Japanese, then the guys of the First made it clear we didn't know anything. Meeting up with them after they had lived through everything we had not was an eerie experience. It was sort of like encountering an older, more knowing, more beat-up, and angrier version of ourselves.

They had the same training as us, were as skilled and fit, and so had every right to believe they were as tough as we felt we were. But they had been through

Guadalcanal. That meant they had lost one-fifth of their men in two months. They had contracted malaria and jungle rot and dysentery. They had killed the enemy in all kinds of ways — long-distance rifle fire, close-up machine gunning that would cut a guy practically in half. Bayonet. Ka-Bar knife across the throat from behind.

They'd also had front row seats at the banzai attacks, where whole companies of Japanese infantry would suddenly rush all at once, screaming and with bayonets raised. Half of us thought those suicide tactics were just myths until we heard firsthand. Now they are our nightmares. It's not just the bloodcurdling sound of the thing, although that would be enough. It's that, when you see it, see them coming faster, closer, there's the awareness that they don't care about dying, not one bit. And while it may not be a strategically wise move to run straight into gunfire, you can't help thinking about what one of these guys will do to you if you're the lucky loser whose gun jams at the wrong time.

Or so they tell us. We are lucky, Second Battalion. We can learn from the experience, without having to get it the hard way.

We even got our own infusion of iron-rich, combat-tested blood. The First Battalion, shot up and laid low as they were, had a lot of realigning to do among their companies and platoons. So somebody had an inspired idea — sounds like a Colonel Krulak move, to be sure — of encouraging some shuffling of personnel between the two battalions. Not a lot, but enough to give a green platoon like mine a permanent battle-hardened presence. Someone who'd been there and could share the knowledge he'd paid dearly for at moments when we would need it most.

There were plenty of guys ready to tell all in the chow line. But that might not be quite enough to keep some of us from getting killed in a foxhole or on a patrol on account of the man with the experience being already in the latrine when he remembered, "Oh, just one more thing, but it's crucial that you keep in mind . . ."

It was strictly voluntary, of course, because nobody wanted to separate guys from their squadron buddies after all they'd been through together. Sadly, it was to our benefit that Guadalcanal had already separated a good number of men from their buddies, and from life on planet Earth.

Corporal Havlicek is our good fortune that came out of a lot of bad. Formerly of the First, he is now our assistant squad leader under Sergeant Silas. He has a very quiet way about him even though sometimes it seems like he's always talking. There is no way he's much older than us, but there is also no way anybody in this platoon will ever stop regarding him the way we do now — which is as a revered and reliable elder statesman, someone we just know will have the answer when we have a question, and will provide it with no bunk whatsoever attached. Even Sergeant Silas treats him like this, and the only time anybody shows even a hint of discomfort with it, it's not Silas but Havlicek who gets a little embarrassed. He's the opposite of all those blowhard non-coms who have to bellow out their importance because otherwise it wouldn't exist. Havlicek has this habit of looking down at the ground when he gets too much raising up for his liking. He waits for it to pass, then looks up when we're all on the same level ground again. He's talked about level ground a lot, by which I think he means below level ground, by which I mean marines laid low and left on Guadalcanal.

It is the first instance I have seen in my time with the US Armed Forces where rank is not monumentally important to the people involved. And while I may still be a very green marine, I do know I should not expect to see it again.

But even officers have to respect the kind of perspective a guy gains when he fights for months in the stink and the muck side by side with his platoon buddies and then returns to camp as a Platoon of One.

He takes every opportunity to school us on what to expect. He's been doing it right along, but as we come closer to live action, he becomes more direct, more urgent and instructional. It's as if he's caught the scent of the battle zone, and the smell brings back more and more specific detail — information that he is determined to impart to us before it's too late.

"Our enemy is fond of night movements, and they're very good at that." Havlicek is addressing us four machine gunners at the bow of the LST. We are approaching the coast of Vella Lavella, and he has come to retrieve us and get us lined up down below to disembark, but not before sharing some final words of wisdom. "You'll gun down scores and scores of them one day, wiping out half their force in a long day's fighting. Then the next morning they'll have mysteriously spawned replacements for most of their casualties, like they were growing these guys in a garden somewhere deep in the jungle. We have to be ready for stealth, because when they're not making fearless but stupid and suicidal banzai charges, they're laying low and silent in every cave and crevice, under every log and up every tree. They consider capture to be dishonor and humiliation and prefer death, especially if they can take some enemy fighters along with them. To a Japanese soldier, death is the only proper end to a fight. Make sure it is his death, not yours. And that sounds obvious, but nothing about these guys is obvious. Half the time you won't see them. They will be three feet in front of you, but all you'll see is a rock, a palm frond . . . or a nest of Japanese riflemen in a pile, already shot up to pulp by a patrol ahead of you. Then you see the muzzle flash . . ."

"Good advice, corporal," I say as I fall in line behind Klecko and Klecko falls in behind Havlicek.

"Yeah," Westphal says from the rear.

"Yeah, thanks," Bryant says from right behind me.

The voices are all sincere, but they are distant. I imagine the guys are preoccupied with the beachhead, as the ship grinds in over the sand and coral, making a frightening growl right beneath the whole lot of us.

And I would also bet they were still hung up on the part of the conversation where the word *banzai* made its appearance.

As the men and machines of the Second Parachute ready for their amphibious assault, the sounds of all the steel gears and chains and plates grind and roar and shriek with effort. It is noise that could be used as its own weapon against less stouthearted warriors than the ones we are about to meet. The last few moments before the drawbridge lowers last ages and ages. Too much. Too much time to think. The nervous chatter of the troops has been replaced with nervous quiet as we do all our chattering and screaming anticipation within the walls of our toughened and fearless marine skulls, behind hard, stoical marine sneers and snarls.

I terrorize my own self with thoughts as I batter that landing ramp down with my mind. We were told by numerous First Battalion vets that the Japanese are not much more likely to take prisoners than they are to become ones. But on the odd occasions when they do, the results are . . . unpleasant.

More than once, a marine from the First started a story about finding the body of a captured buddy, and then couldn't finish it. And since they had managed to tell us about beheadings, I could hardly imagine what they found unspeakable.

If this ramp does not fall open within four seconds I'm afraid I will in fact start to imagine the unimaginable unspeakable. Whether these tales were designed to make us well educated or well terrified, I can report that they accomplished both. At least in my case.

I wouldn't blame those guys if they had come limping

back to New Caledonia feeling like they'd already done a whole war's worth of their part. If it was me, I think I'd be happy to just lie in a hammock in the Solomons sunshine for a while rather than do any more training, learn any more art of warfare. Yet they have matched our energy and determination at every turn. During these last few months we've pushed one another further and higher, meaner and harder, through hand-to-hand . . . to-hand-to-hand combat drills. We practiced the things we now knew we had to master, like jungle fighting, night operations, and amphibious beach landings in rubber craft and flat-bottomed Higgins boats. We continued our practice jumps as often as we could get the aircraft to jump from, but that, frankly, was not often enough. The Marine Corps itself has far too few planes of our own, and we have learned that the rivalry between us and the Army was just as real as the banzai attacks and potentially just as lethal. They managed to lend us the transport aircraft we needed just enough times that we made twenty or so jumps the whole time we were at Camp Kiser. That included six nighttime jumps, which were exciting and more than a little unnerving as we leaped, literally blindly, into the unknown.

More and more, the planes we needed were assigned to resupplying hot spots like Guadalcanal, so opportunities dwindled. The final jump we made, it was clearly an inexperienced and disinterested pilot they sent to take us out, and the result was a disaster. He flew us toward the drop zone from an awkward approach, came in too low and too close to the highlands. Guys wound up landing hard, landing hurt, landing nowhere near where they were supposed to be and in many cases nowhere near each other. The final jumper was a private first class whose first or last name was George and was so shy I never heard what his voice sounded like. The Army pilot was so confused and hurried that he was pulling up and gaining altitude before George could make a proper exit. So the kid just dove out of the plane before it could get any higher.

He slammed into the side of a jagged cliff almost as soon as his chute opened, and they said his body was already lifeless as it bounced and flopped and jack-knifed and skidded along several hundred feet of raw hillside.

This somehow, through Army logic, must have proved that their planes should be doing other things. Because with the death of Private First Class George, we never saw another Army aircraft on New Caledonia.

Colonel Krulak, our commanding officer, seemed to sense a turning point in this, and probably even before this. Because he trained us on land ever harder, harder and harder, as if we were commandos. We might sometime be dropped into a battle zone from the sky, or we might get there via land or sea. But Colonel Krulak was making sure that once we got there we were going to be prepared to work behind enemy lines, to operate as guerillas, to act as advance scouts on reconnaissance patrols, to fight as attachments to a division, or to fight without any attachments to anybody. We would be experts at packing our own parachutes, and at driving the Ka-Bar between a man's ribs with the right placement and force to ensure maximum blood loss and swiftest death. The colonel had every one of us ready to kill with a gun, or a grenade, or a rock, or a thumb dug in deep behind an eye and into a brain, if necessary.

To do basically *anything*, if necessary.

We might or might not be paratroopers, but we would definitely be raiders.

So we are ready. We're ready for this, and we're ready right now, and it's only the refusal of that big slab of steel to open up and slap down in the water that we need to fear at this moment. I fear also that I might now scream and holler from the sheer unbearable crazy of it all, and forever mark myself as *that* guy among true marines.

When the LST finally opens with a great grinding thud onto Vella Lavella and the bow of the ship is replaced by the golden road before us, we march down the ramp and up the beach looking like a seasoned bunch of career marines who know just what they're doing and who fear no one.

I can't tell about everybody else, but my heart is banging away as if I have my own drum corps accompaniment working from within my chest and on out through my ears. I have my machine gun up and ready as I scan the small strip of sand that leads immediately into a jungle dense enough to provide its own permanent nighttime. I'm expecting, as I think we all are, some kind of hostile greeting for our party, but there is nothing coming, not a shot, before our guys start filing in along the narrow paths that lead to the island's interior. I'd almost rather be shot at than enter the thick of the place this quick and easy.

We are orderly, as precise as well-drilled marines should be while we march in step, in rhythm, in lines that cut right into the trails.

"You all right, buddy?" I say to Klecko, who is just ahead of me and utterly silent. "Zachary?" I say as he just grimly forges ahead.

Then, his one remark as we submerge ourselves in aromatic vegetation and walk through the door separating day from night: "Ants. Just like I said. We're ants."

Ah, he could always make me laugh. Right now it's a relief to hear any small such thing to connect us to that world and who we really are. When it gets so tense and creepy silent, I fear I could forget.

I squeeze my M55 Reising submachine gun as I step higher to keep from tripping up in the dense undergrowth. I make a rapid mental circuit of my gear belt, taking note of where everything is: canteen — since my mouth is already sandpaper-dry — ammunition, and especially my knife.

The trail of ants stretches from our lead man, who's now a couple hundred yards deep into the heart of Vella Lavella, all the way back to the LST, where troops are still filing out and tons of supplies are being unloaded. Then the thick Solomons air is ruffled by the first distinct rumblings of aircraft approaching from the forward distance. Those first rumblings then grow to a terrible roar as the planes close in at an alarming pace. The peace is finally good and shattered by the screech of the whistle signaling everybody to head for cover.

We look like a desperate marine version of a Hollywood dance number gone very wrong. Every man dives headlong off the narrow footpath and into the thick brush on either side. Left-right-left-right-left, we seem to hurl ourselves in an alternating sequence as if we've planned it that way.

But we did not plan anything beyond answering the whistle by hurling ourselves as forcefully as possible, face-first and out of harm's way. That proves plan enough, however, as the machine guns of the fighter plane tear up the path, all the way up his head-on approach. The strafing passes us just as we've leapt, so close I can feel the fabric of my pant legs flapping with the whoosh of the bullets buzzing by while I'm still in mid-dive.

Before we can catch a breath, a second fighter comes right behind the first, swoops down even lower, and peppers the earth all around us with hundreds of rounds that are heavy enough to create a miniature earthquake in the ground we're all clinging to.

I think I'd be petrified even if they left the bullets out of it. The sound of those brutal birds bearing down on you and causing your internal organs to vibrate and bash into each other is probably enough to kill people who don't happen to be US Marines, right there on the spot. We are one of the rare outfits that trained often with live ammo, but even all that cannot prepare a guy for the force generated by an enemy dive bomber bearing down on him, engines roaring and guns banging loud and relentless.

Never felt anywhere near so puny and helpless in my whole life. And we're just getting started.

"You all right, buddy?" Klecko says from his spot flat on the ground six feet ahead.

"I believe I am. You?"

"I think so. But man, if that racket doesn't stop a person's heart cold, I don't figure there's gonna be anything else we can't shake off, huh?"

"You probably don't want to start letting yourself think that way," Corporal Havlicek says. He's on his feet now, standing over Klecko but watching the dogfight taking place over the beach. The two Japanese bombers clearly want to see pieces of LST scattered across the Pacific before they leave again. The boys on the ship are giving them everything they've got, pounding away with the thunderous antiaircraft guns, which don't score but do drive the two bombers off their course and into a big sweep of a second approach.

Corporal Havlicek marches past me on the path back toward the beach. Sergeant Silas is right behind him and the rest of us fall in.

We just reach the jungle's edge again when the shock of daylight is overruled by a far bigger shock to the senses. Two more of the dive bombers come screaming over the back of us, with two Marine Corps Corsairs right on their tails, blistering them with machine-gun fire that is too relentless to escape.

We watch the whole show unfold, as guys scramble madly to get off the ship. The two later bombers veer off out over the sea, taking the two Corsairs with them. One of the first bombers almost clips a Corsair's tail as he comes scorching back in, through an explosive shower of antiaircraft fire. He ignores it as he homes in on the ship and drops his package. It looks like a big black oil drum, and it is so unlike a torpedo or anything you expect to see a warplane dumping, that there's a strange, static moment of nothing as the thing descends. The bomber has already banked and headed out of there before the oil drum finally crashes down on our LST.

It is no oil drum, of course. It's a five-hundred-pound bomb, and the explosion is so massive it knocks most of us right off our feet from more than a football field away.

I'm sitting flat on my backside as I try to take in the sight of the ship breaking and burning. The backdrop to this grisly picture is the final scene of the Corsairs finishing off the two bombers. Our guys do everything but follow the two flaming Japanese aircraft all the way into the water to see to it that they're gone before pulling out of their dive and swooping back this way. They make one pass over the wreckage and mayhem and then scorch off across the sky toward some other crisis they might actually be able to do something about.

Because this is not it.

We stay down for cover long enough for the threat to appear over for the lucky ones like us. Then the sergeant gives us the word to head down closer to the scene.

The awesome, mighty giant that just so recently coughed us up onto this sand is now a colossal heap of blown-apart metal and men, fire shooting straight up ahead of black smoke, making me think about how they talked in church about the soul escaping the dead body.

The personnel who were close to the ship have been thrown high and far and in every direction. The guys who were almost away, still hustling down the ramp, were unluckier still. I've heard people use that term "blown apart," an exaggeration that has meant lots of stupid things. But the guys too close to the explosion got blown apart. We can see it before we can believe it, limbs, pulpy pieces of stuff that have to be human, were human seconds before, flung like pig slop across the beach and into the water. The guys from the ramp came apart in bits that were actually still on fire as they sailed. The guys inside . . .

We don't get any closer than fifty feet from the wreck. The Navy corpsmen are doing what they do and it is now for us to stay out of their way and do what we do.

"Let's march, marines," Havlicek calls out after waiting long enough for Silas to not do it. Couldn't blame the sarge for lingering. Couldn't blame anybody.

We listen, and obey orders. That's something we're renowned for. Back in file, stepping sharply, we take to that same trail we were taking, to go do the job we're meant to be doing.

Picking up right where we left off, just like nothing ever happened.

"Now, where were we?" Bryant says right behind me, with an edgy growl-laugh after.

"Who cares?" I say, pretty much the same way. "Where *are* we, that's what I'm wonderin' about. And where are we goin'?"

CHAPTER FIVE

Are We There Yet?

Vella Lavella turns out not to be the big debut a lot of us were hoping it would be.

The answer to my question about where we are going, at least in the immediate and literal sense, is Barakoma Airfield. We aren't here to capture it, because that has already been done. The Japanese had occupied the island early in the war, and three years later our military bosses suddenly decided they would quite like to have it back, as part of some bigger scheme. So take it back is what our boys did, with the assistance of the New Zealanders, and to my surprise they are all still hanging around the place, instead of the hordes of furious Japanese I was expecting to meet.

So we are here simply to act as guards for Barakoma and the modest area of land we possess around it. That's all. There are still pockets of Japanese troops holding out and hiding out here and there on the island, but you wouldn't even call it resistance. Aside from constant dogfighting in the sky — which is the case all over this area of operations — the only small portion of Vella Lavella that anybody is even bothered to fight over is the tiny little airstrip.

Kind of makes me sad to think about it. How militaries come in warring like madmen over some tiny plunk of a place in the great wide ocean, a perfectly nice little island that's been sitting there minding its own business for thousands of years. Then, at some point they're just gonna throw it away again like it never mattered anyway. It's stupid, of course. There are a lot of things happening and gonna happen that deserve my sadness more than Vella Lavella.

Anyway, we marines of the Second Parachute Battalion didn't fight for it, either. This was no raid, no invasion, no assault-by-sea. We are to babysit the airstrip until it's somebody else's turn. And we are to go on regular patrols just to make sure the random armed-and-dangerous Japanese fighter doesn't get frisky thinking that nobody's paying any attention. And we wait, still wait, for somebody to ask us to join in the real fighting. The stuff we trained for. The stuff that matters.

"Everything matters, though," Klecko points out when we head out on our evening patrol. It's a four-man detail with Bryant and Westphal along for the comradeship and the guns. We have done several of these, and though I know better, I can't help letting my focus go soft some of the time. Vigilance is key to not getting killed, especially at the quietest times. But there are only so many tours you can make of one very small volcanic islet without it lulling you somewhat.

Unless you are intrepid Private First Class Zachary Klecko, USMC. Gotta give him credit, the boy lulls not. He is unlullable, and treats every twig on the jungle floor and every tropical flower blooming horizontally out of a hill as if it just might be the one that is hiding *that* soldier. Hiding the soldier who is holding the grenade that just might have our names on it.

"It all matters, sure," I say, clapping my buddy on the shoulder. He is startled up out of his night-patrol crouch, and wheels on me in a way I hope no enemy ever does.

"Don't *do* that, Nardini, all right?" he snarls at me.

"Sorry," I say, truly sorry when I see how bothered he is. The other two dissolve in a flurry of laughs that flies right off on the soft evening breeze when he glowers at them.

"Eighteen guys got killed coming here," Klecko says as he resumes patrolling. "Our guys, our battalion.

That's got to matter, doesn't it? So maybe you don't get why we're here, and maybe I don't, and maybe none of those dead guys exactly knew, either, but so what. You're either all in or all out, dontcha think? If you're only gonna go along with the orders you completely understand you're not much of a marine, then, are ya?"

We are standing at one of the highest points on the island, a clear patch that allows a great view pretty much all the way back to Hawaii on a good day. It's already too dark to see much, with these south central Pacific sunsets that drop on you like a curtain ending the show for today. We're set to descend down the back side of our patrol area, back into the forest of true darkness, but we can pause and take a few more swigs of mountaintop air before we do.

"Ah, you're right, Klecko, man," Westphal says, offering a tap of the barrel of his gun like a toast.

"Yeah, of course you are," Bryant says, adding his gun nozzle to the toast.

Feeling pretty clearly isolated now, I rush to add my gun to what now must look like four guys holding up an automatic weaponry Christmas tree on a peak for the whole world's pleasure.

"Right," Klecko says, breaking up the party and leading the way down, "for example, if I needed to understand what the brass were thinking all the time, then I sure wouldn't be going to war with this mangy little thing, would I?" He's waving his Reising M55 submachine gun over his head, and all of us, carrying the very same weapon, groan and laugh at the same time. "Come on now, Nicky, remember summer camp. I swear to you we could have made these things ourselves, at Camp Agassis, when we were nine."

He has got a strong point, which is why we are all laughing along as he says it. To be fair, we are built to be a lightly armed, nimble, and creative invasion force. Quick hits, getting behind enemy lines, taking beaches but not *keeping* them — that's what we are all about. Then we hand over the keys to the Army, infantry guys with the heavier armaments, and head off to our next hit-and-run conquest.

I know before I even try that he won't be buying any debate, but I give it a try anyway.

"Lightly armed, Private Klecko . . . a mobile and nimble invasion force —"

"Does this look like any kind of force to you?" Zack says. He takes his M55 and starts swinging it around and around over his head. The firearm is distinctive for, among other things, having no solid, wooden stock like most submachine guns. It has a sort of outline of a stock, molded out of what seems to be a heavy-duty coat hanger. My buddy Klecko, the gunner to whom I am just an assistant, has slipped the wire-frame stock around his wrist like a bracelet, and is giving it enough propeller motion that he could soon start gaining altitude.

The guys, of course, love it, and are cracking up, following along in the big gunner man's wake.

I don't even know why I look in the direction I do then.

I don't know how it catches my eye, why it ever would, even if I were paying strict attention like we should do when on patrol. I am certain I would never catch something like this, so small, so blended into the growth around the base of that tree, if I were looking hard and trying to catch such a thing. A sandal, so perfect for the job of blending in that it could have been made out of the bark of the very tree that shields the man who wears it.

PrrrrRuttaTuttaTuttaTuttPrrrRuttaTuttaTutt

The smell of the smoke, off the gunpowder and the flash-heated oil from the gun — because I do take superb care of my weapon whatever it is — instantly adds its tang to the special particular scent of this bitty island, this clearing in this jungle on this dot in the crazy vast expanse of the Pacific Ocean. Instantly it adds, and instantly it changes it. Changes the scent into something entirely different now.

Westphal is the one who first approaches the body. He creeps up on it slowly, one extended ballet step forward followed by another and another. We have heard all about the booby-trapped bodies of dead Japanese snipers. They are only too happy to die if they know their American killer will be following right after them. We all have our sad M55s poised as we fan out around Westphal, covering his back, as well as the tree branches above him, and every flicker of insect business on every leaf all around him. Westphal finally pokes his gun barrel into the dead man's side, pokes him, pokes him harder, then uses the gun as a lever to pry him partly away from the ground. Have to make sure there are no smaller and more-alive assassins underneath ready to finish the job.

"I think we're clear," he says, which is the word that lets the rest of us stop scouring the area like a team of lightly armed owls.

"You sure he's dead-dead?" Bryant asks for all of us, because stories are rampant of Japanese dead on the field who turn out not to be dead-dead. Who then spring up to knife a clueless and careless GI to death-death.

"Pretty sure, yeah," Westphal says. He leans toward our former enemy and repeats the same prying move, using his gun barrel to lift and then this time turn the guy over. Or more accurately, he turns the guy's top half over. The guy lies there, facedown but with his hips still aimed toward the sky. This is my first real look at him, and it's only too obvious. There are pulpy pieces of his tissue sprayed in a random pattern behind the body; his midsection was essentially torn away by the steady and concentrated slash of bullets I laid back and forth across his body. The blood is pooling, the insects of the forest are gathering, and the scent of Vella Lavella is changing again.

Bryant suddenly starts gagging, runs to a cluster of trees where he pukes like a flamethrower. I walk closer to the man, the man I just killed, the first man I have killed.

His feet are very sad. It was those feet in those sandals that caught my eye to begin with. Well, one of the feet, extending just an inch or two too far beyond the tree's few visible roots. Small mistakes in this. Small mistakes will be enough.

His feet in those sandals are at an awkward, unnatural angle to each other, and it's upsetting me. I know that his upper body is at a far more unnatural angle to the rest of him and that should be the disturbing thing, and I don't know why but that isn't of interest to me. Both feet are pointed a little inward, while his legs are splayed as if he is in mid-stride of a very pathetic run. The toes peeking from his left sandal are pointing back over where his right shoulder should be. His right foot is locked in a painful-looking arrangement, pigeon-toed and twisted almost backward at the ankle and digging into the forest floor.

Bryant has just about finished heaving and is headed our way when I go over and realign the man's feet in his very modest sandals. I face them the right way and then tuck them close together. I stop to look him over, and someone has realigned his other stuff, too, and I didn't even notice.

The four of us walk in a fairly tight two-by-two formation down the hill, through the jungle land, toward camp.

"I just hope somebody would straighten out my feet when the time comes," I say, answering a question I now don't think anybody was going to ask. "Not leave me lying there all bent up and stupid-looking like that."

"Sure," Bryant says from behind me. I think he's just not ready for multi-syllable words yet.

"You saved my life, Nick," Klecko says, walking almost nonregulation close to having his shoulder touching mine.

"I did, yeah," I say, and it does not feel like bragging, because it does not feel like anything.

Westphal is carrying the Japanese rifle, going over it, checking out the features, the balance, the heft. "Now this is a real gun," he says, not quite achieving admiration for anything Japanese, but near enough for him. "But hey, I think maybe we were a bit unkind about the trusty little M55 earlier, huh? Maybe it has got some kicks in it."

"Kicks," Klecko says flatly.

"Lots of kicks," I say, still feeling the buzzing in my fingers, which is different from the buzzing in my head, or my guts, or my feet.

CHAPTER SIX

We're with The Brute

For eighteen days Vella Lavella is our place of business, and it is our home. I am aching to get away from the island and it's got to be soon. If I don't get away via official deployment then I am just about ready to go the Alcatraz route and take my chances with the cruel ocean tides calling from every direction I look.

Stupid as it sounds, I don't believe I gave much thought at all to what it would feel like to kill a man. I suppose I figured it would be . . . less personal. Like in movies, where guys get shot all the time. No hard feelings, fella. That's why we have guns. To keep our distance. To keep us removed. So we can go about our business. So we can kill *enemy fighters*, not people. Not people, with feet and sandals and maybe little people of their own at home, in little bitty sandals, waiting for him to come back.

The smell, it hasn't gone away. Not since that moment when the scents of this place and everything that's happening all merged up into this awful stinger of an odor that I can't escape from. It's like a dented fender from a close-call crash in your cheap old jalopy, or a broken, crooked nose that never healed right, or a crack widening in the foundation of your house a little bit at a time. I've had all those things, lived with them without ever growing fond of them, and I've done all right. The smell — which I have been thinking of as *Smella Lavella* just to lighten it up, grab a smile wherever I can — the smell, I guess, is gonna be like those things. Things that come to you uninvited, stick around, and never leave, and you get used to them over time.

I will, over time. For now, though, whenever I close my eyes I feel like I'm in a foxhole with a bloody, pulpy dead guy pressed up against me. Because that's what my dreams have told me to feel, and that's why sleep ain't no friend of mine at the moment. So I wait anxiously for a combat assignment to get me off this lump and then see how I do. Otherwise, those tides are always there.

But now, just now, there's a competing tide washing right over our camp here. Rumors are strong that genuine action is about to come our way. Commander of the battalion has been summoned to the headquarters of First Marine Amphibious Corps (IMAC) on Guadalcanal. It's a move that almost certainly signals a real deployment, and an important task. Knowing the kind of faith the commander has in us, there is no way he's leaving IMAC headquarters without some great nasty invasion plan clutched in his fist, or, for the sake of security, stashed elsewhere on his small but rugged person.

Lieutenant Colonel Victor Krulak was not the original commander of the Second Marine Parachute Battalion. We were already at New Caledonia when he came along. At every level, I felt, we had received top-grade instruction and conditioning no matter who was leading us. So the battalion Colonel Krulak found at Camp Kiser was physically rock-hard, and mentally quite well educated on the subject of soldiering.

That was combined, though, with a bit of unruliness creeping in as a direct result of our frustration over being left out of battle month after month. All the while, marines were leaving their guts on beaches and battlefields all over the world. What should you expect if you train a specially selected population of motivated young men to the point where they are up to the job of taking on any army you got, are dying to do so, but are kept cooped up with just each other to engage in hostilities with? I'd say they should be happy we didn't blow right past unruliness and head straight for open violence and general mayhem.

We were more than frustrated. We were insulted over not being asked to fight. And we were ashamed at the burden being carried by others while we sat.

What I appreciated right off about the colonel was that he liked what he found with us. Sure, we needed discipline, but Victor "Brute" Krulak understood why we were itchin', even admired us for feeling that way. He knew what to do from day one. It's my guess that with him being a complete green-blooded US Marine as committed to the Corps as anybody all the way up the pole, he probably already saw the writing on the wall that the Marine Parachute Regiments weren't ever going to jump into a live battle. The rivalry between us and the Army was already hot and the flame went higher every time the Marines made the news for being spectacular and heroic while the Army just always plugged along being pretty ordinary. Scuttlebutt was that the Marines' heroics on Guadalcanal and in the newspapers had gotten top Army brass so steamed up that we'd never set foot on another of their transport planes — which the jumps would require — even if we bought every one of our guys a full fare ticket two weeks in advance and returned the aircraft washed and waxed and loaded up with fresh-baked oatmeal cookies.

To be fair, I can understand why they might feel

about us the way they do. I'd be jealous and resentful of the Marines, too, if I was stuck in the Army. We should probably include the Navy while we're at it. They don't care for us much, either.

By the time he took the reins at Fort Kiser, Brute Krulak, all five-foot-five and 130 pounds of mean green marine, would not only have been up on these matters of interservice feuding; listening to him talk, it was a fair bet he was an active and enthusiastic part of it.

Therefore, while we never neglected our jump training when it was possible, the methods, tactics, and intensity Colonel Krulak brought to his training regime all seemed designed to keep us in the game in the event that our defining element — parachuting — was going to be denied us by forces beyond our control. He was going to put on the field a band of special forces that would be the equal of those any other nation could boast. Including and especially the US Army's famous Rangers.

"It's more than just the Army being petty with us, though," Sergeant Silas says as the bunch of us walk together. We're about to hear the big announcement Colonel Krulak has brought back for us all.

"What else is there?" I ask.

"Well, 'what else' is that paratroops and this campaign were never going to be a good fit. All those pint-size islands, landing zones almost nonexistent . . ."

"You've seen the density of the jungle terrain here," Corporal Havlicek interjects. "Well, I can tell you, it's all uphill from Vella Lavella. That's not the kind of canopy a paratrooper jumps through; it's the kind he bounces off of, and lands back on the beach with everybody else anyway."

I open my mouth to counter, but I can't think of anything.

"It would be terrific to get a real chance," Silas adds, "and this outfit would be exceptional at it. But the cold fact is, no special unit in the world can jump behind enemy lines if there are no enemy lines to be found."

The more I hear the more obviously right this argument becomes. And the more grateful I am that Colonel Krulak had the foresight to turn us into a commando unit without even bothering to tell anybody what he was really up to.

We file into the big mess tent that will just about accommodate the entire six-hundred-and-fifty-strong battalion. It's an odd moment, trying to fit us all in at the same time. Makes me realize this is one of the very few times the entire unit has been called together for anything like this. One more reason to expect something big's up.

We're among the more conscientious — or more anxious — squads, who get here early and quickly fill up all the dining tables and chairs. The next wave take all the spots around the edges. It's cozy enough that I hope the stragglers will be reasonable and just hover around outside to listen. There are plenty of screen windows if they want to look on as the colonel speaks. And as for being able to hear Brute Krulak from that distance, talking over the several hundred blocky heads shouldn't prove to be an obstacle for him.

In the meantime, there is lots of low murmuring, chatter, and laughter among the troops, all steadily increasing in volume the longer we wait for the main event. The frenzy that could build here is as likely as not to be something the man himself is engineering. A rabid audience would most likely suit him.

Across the table, I notice Klecko is at it again. He is staring *the* stare that was born in this place just this week and is one of the many things I hope we leave behind when we escape this wretched rock. If Krulak comes out and announces that they're asking for volunteers to parachute down into a live volcano, I'll be the first guy with his hand in the air. This lump of lava we're on now feels like it's haunted, and Klecko and I both feel it.

I lean across and tap his elbow. "Zack, man, please, how many times already have I asked you not to do that? Knock it off with that thing, really, or I'm gonna wind up as demented as you. We don't want to get sent home like *that*, do we? Cripes, the jerks in the Eastern Shore League would have me for lunch. They'd rag me so bad I'd never be able to hit real pitching again. You want that to happen to me? After all I've done for you?"

Oh, jeez, why'd I have to go and say *that*?

"Scratch that. We do for each other and always have. But, I told you, Zachary, I don't want to talk about any of it. You're alive, I'm alive, there's a war on, y'know, so we'll take being alive as a pretty good state of affairs. And just not talk anymore about who killed or didn't kill who, right? Right? Now buck up, kid, we're gonna be great. First step is we're getting outta here, and we're goin' to a fight. That's the perfect start right there." The whole place stirs as The Brute makes his entrance. "And here, here he is, so very soon we will know. I'm already packed, how 'bout you?"

He gives me the tilted-head look, like when you try to explain the infield fly rule to a dog.

"No, I'm not packed yet, Nick. No matter what the

colonel tells us today, we'll still have time to pack up properly. You sure, though? That you're gonna be able to get on with things, with whatever we gotta do, once you leave Vella and everything behind?"

"I don't know," I say wearily. I don't even look at him but focus on our commanding officer smiling broadly and wrestling the podium out of his way.

"You killed somebody, Nicky. And you had to do it because I stopped being a soldier and started being a clown. Unforgiveable. I even think that sniper came up specifically for me, because what a fool I was. We passed that spot maybe two dozen times on patrols and he was happy just layin' low until his men came and evacuated him to some other island. Like they already did for so many other guys. But I raised him up, right out of the ground, because I was so childish, so dishonorable, acting as if there was no danger, acting like he and his comrades were nothing. Acting like, hey, Mr. Enemy, have a look at the nation of oafs who are invading all your islands and killing you left and right. That was all my fault, all of it, and it is beneath the dignity of every marine who ever suited up. Conflict is serious. War, and the people who fight it, are serious. The people we fight it *for* are serious. How can I tell Rosie how close I already came to dying, and how come? She made me promise to do my job but not do anything foolish because I gotta get home in the end."

This actually provides me with one of those hard-to-come-by smiles.

"I imagine she was thinking about foolish hero stuff like throwing yourself on live grenades, or storming a hill full of Japanese gun nests all by yourself . . ."

"Oh, and not, *Don't forget to not act like a big dope and dance around on patrol and make yourself look like a juicy fat duck in a shooting gallery just for the lonely Japanese sniper*? You think she probably hadn't anticipated that one, huh?"

My small smile has slipped away. "Do you suppose he was? Lonely?"

"Arrrr," Klecko says in frustration, grabbing fistfuls of his own hair tightly. "You, buddy, best pal o' mine, you surely figured you were gonna have to kill somebody eventually, no? This great big adventure, shoved into motion by you alone." He looks at me like he's worried he said the wrong thing. "Except, of course, it's never you alone. It never will be, either. Buddy system, right to the end. We won't get separated, no matter what. And when we cross that finish line we'll go all the way back to that wise-guy recruiting officer together and say, see, pal, now this is a real buddy system you're lookin' at."

"Buddy system," I say. "We'll be great. It's just taking some adjustment."

Klecko nods because he understands, because he always has and that's why he's here.

Except I don't really believe anybody can understand this. Until it's their turn.

For now, I am grateful for the understanding nod that will have to do until my adjustment sets in, like it surely will.

And with any luck it starts right here . . .

"I have some good news for you," The Brute bellows, louder than any five-and-a-half-foot unamplified lieutenant colonel in history. "Our long wait is over. Our battalion has its mission — and it is a mission for which we have been specially chosen because only we have the expertise to pull it off. General Vandegrift himself told me that Second Battalion is the best-trained outfit in the South Pacific, and if you ask me, the general is in this case showing a tendency toward understatement."

We are as disciplined a group of men as has ever existed. But you'd be forgiven for thinking otherwise during the long stretch of raucous, earsplitting, throat-tearing noise that follows.

The Brute allows us our noise, until he doesn't. When he raises his hand, the silence that follows is absolute.

"Our target is Choiseul Island, currently home to some five thousand enemy troops. They will have the numbers, and furthermore, they will know we are there. Soon after we make our landing on what our coast-watchers assure us is an unguarded beach, the Marine Corps will announce to the United States media that twenty thousand marines have landed on Choiseul. We know the Japanese are watching our news reports, and we know that they have so far been able to rely upon what they learn there. That reliance is going to cost them. But if our single battalion is going to pull this off, we are going to have to make some noise on that island. Can we do that?"

Can we ever. Can we ever make some noise. We give him just a little preview of it now.

The Brute, somehow, is able to speak over all six hundred and fifty of us.

"While we engage the enemy on Choiseul," he roars, "our brothers in the Third Marine Division will be landing at Bougainville. Every Japanese soldier we draw away from the invasion of Bougainville is a Japanese soldier who cannot shoot those men. If our diversion is successful, we save marine lives. No mission is more important than that, and I can think of no greater honor."

It comes as no surprise that Krulak is as adept with spirited public speaking as he is with a bayonet. As he continues his address, he gets all the guys roaring and stamping their feet several times. Even one very serious point he feels the need to stress more than once brings only cheers. "We will be on our own in the realest sense. We will have the PT boat base and air cover, both from Vella Lavella, but that is all the backup we are going to get, regardless of what we run into."

Roars for the words *on our own*. More roars for the Patrol Torpedo boat crews we've gotten to know somewhat during endless patrols around Vella. Good guys all around, including one skipper, a lieutenant whose father is supposed to be America's ambassador to Great Britain, according to scuttlebutt. Could be true, since Lieutenant Kennedy kinda looks like he could be the ambassador himself. If he ever put a shirt on, anyway.

The Brute even wraps up his address by showing that his skills extend to death-based comedy tucked neatly within useful practical advice. "Snipers will be targeting the men in charge, so don't go around addressing officers by rank out there. If you want a fast and short-lived promotion, just call me colonel, I will call you general right back."

At the end there's no stomping only because every last marine is already on his feet, clapping, whistling, and looking for all the world like we'll be charging straight to the boats to start this thing right now.

But Zack was right, as he tends to be when over-excitement threatens to carry things away. We will have a few days to prepare.

Our platoon holds back while the rest of the crowd rowdy-files out into the evening. We remain seated at our long table like some board of directors clearing the room for top-level business.

"So," Sergeant Silas begins, "what do we think of what we just heard?"

"Are we even sure what we just heard?" Larry Seigfreid asks. Larry is a good guy and smart like a science professor. He is one of our two genius demolition experts, along with Mal Graham, who is just as smart. They speak infrequently, and mostly to each other. They sure know their explosives, though, and every other kind of chemistry, apparently. The two of them spend their free time actually devising their own invented demolition devices from every discarded scrap or surplus kit that has anything dangerous left in it at all. Truth is, I can almost never make heads or tails out of them, and I was more than happy to tell them that on several occasions. It's how they got their nicknames, Seigfreid being a good sport and going along with being "Heads," while Graham, I suppose understandably, took longer to warm up to "Tails."

"I was thinking that, too," Tails says. "I mean, what is it all about? Is it a real raid, or a phony?"

"What difference does it make?" Westphal says. "As long as we get to shoot 'em up and Heads and Tails get to blow 'em up, that's all the ball game you need right there as far as I'm concerned."

Westphal's angle sounds a lot like the "we don't need to understand everything" approach Klecko was talking about just before The Incident. I look in his direction and give him a nod. He gives me a nod right back and things feel like they're creeping in the right direction, at least momentarily.

Tom Chaney is one of our two demolition men who are of ordinary intelligence, with Sandy Satchel being the other. These two are in the demo business for the same reason most of us would be: because they just love making things go boom-fall-down and don't waste any brain cells wondering how any of it works.

"Pretty good speech, whatever it was," Chaney says.

"Oh yeah," Satchel says. "Halfway through Brute's pep talk I was all ready to go out and enlist, before I remembered I was already in."

Bryant jumps in. "Colonel Brute might have been just preaching to the choir, but even if he was, he sure knows the music."

"That he does," Silas says. "That he does."

"What about you, Private Silence?" Havlicek calls to me as the guys are all getting up to go. I'm already praying that that name doesn't stick. "Did you hear the words you came hoping to hear? Does the work ahead of us sound like the kind of fighting that *matters*?"

It's on the scary side, when you notice just how tuned in Corporal Havlicek seems to be to all the happenings and all the personalities that make up this battalion life. Scary or not, though, I always feel that I want to give him the honest answers his honest questions deserve.

"I have a strong sense that what we are about to embark on matters very much and is important work, corporal," I say firmly and respectfully.

He nods in my direction and smiles in a knowing, satisfied way, while the rest of the men start letting me have it.

"Oh, right, fellas, we can go to Choiseul now," Bryant cackles, "because Private Silence says it's okay."

He yuck-yucks away at his own joke, which would be extremely bad form, if everybody else wasn't hooting right along with him.

"No, no, no," Westphal says. "He never told us it was okay, he told us it was . . ."

"Im-POR-tant!" every last laughing rat in the whole platoon yells as one.

They are still falling over each other, banging their way out the door as I make every effort to punish them. But they're completely ignoring the withering glare that I normally reserve only for pitchers who think they own the inner half of the plate when I'm at bat, and catchers who try and block that same plate when I'm barreling in to score.

Me oh my, how much I miss baseball now.

I don't know which stare I have on my face now, where I'm aiming, or how long I've been at it. But machine gunner Zachary Klecko has just dropped a big paw on the shoulder of his assistant gunner, and this is where I am now. In the war, all in, and with my buddy every step.

"We came this far," he says. "Nobody's gonna stop us now. And nobody's gonna split us up. Not even you."

So I guess I've been served notice that there will be no more moping around, or else.

"You know, it just occurred to me," I say, heading

out of the empty mess hall and into the empty, endless night. "You and the Marine Corps have the same motto. *Semper Fidelis*."

"Always faithful! Of course I know that. I had it first. They came and asked if they could borrow it, and I was very gracious about the whole thing and said sure."

"Good of you."

"Well, that's the kinda guy I am. Good."

The conversation carries on more or less just like that, until we reach our tent, which we share with our machine-gunning brethren Bryant and Westphal. Klecko and I are quiet and, speaking for myself, anyway, somehow both wiped out and wound up thinking about the Choiseul assignment. We hunker right down to needed rest.

"*Semper Fi*, Nick," he hush-calls across the tent to me.

"*Semper Fi*, Zachary," I respond.

There is a pause of a very few seconds before "*Semper Fi*, guys," wafts up from the vicinity of Bryant's cot, followed by "*Semper Fi*, men," from Westphal's.

I drift off smiling inwardly and possibly outwardly at our updated version of "good night." I'm thinking maybe there could be at least one extremely positive thing to come out of the war. That would be if we discover that the peculiar, particular something that makes Klecko Klecko turns out to be contagious.

CHAPTER SEVEN

Bliss

In a gesture to maybe make up for leaving us behind for so much of the war, the Corps and Navy send us into Choiseul on a fleet of four destroyer transports, marking a definite step up in class and menace from everything that has carried us previously. And these transports are jacked up even further with the addition of six regular destroyers serving as escorts.

It is all adding up now to something important, which is something this outfit needs. The brass finally seems to understand that. They practically read the thoughts of our battle-starved battalion when they code-named the mission "Operation Blissful."

That all contributes to the general confidence we as a unit carry into our landing at Voza behind Colonel Krulak. Though if you're being led by The Brute and your confidence is still AWOL, then you should probably just stay back on the boat.

One of the Australian coastwatchers who've been helping out as scouts and native liaisons all over these islands is supposed to shine a light to signal that we will get no opposition. When he doesn't as we near land, things get more tense and we gear up for resistance right from the start. Yet when we hit the beach looking for a certain kind of trouble, that trouble seems to have managed to elude us one more time. We land unimpeded, and immediately we're on the move with our fifty-pound packs on our backs.

The beach at Voza sits at about the midpoint between our main interests of Choiseul Bay up at the northwest end of the island and Sangigai down in the southeast. There is enough moonlight to see the expanse of pretty white-sand beach for some distance in each direction and a scattering of thatch-roof huts big enough for people to live in. I wonder what they make of the likes of us tromping right through their paradise of a front yard.

That strikes me as funny for half a second.

People *live* here?

People live here?

But there isn't time to admire beaches or dwell on the mixed luck of the people who live on them. We march, platoon by platoon, one hundred and fifty yards straight from the sea to the tree line that welcomes us to the jungle of Choiseul.

Except that it doesn't. Welcome us, that is. This jungle is at least twice as dense as what we found on Vella Lavella, and we have to fight our way through every foot of it in order to make any progress at all.

"This is what we wanted," Klecko says as he pushes his way into the relentless lushness just ahead of me.

"This is what we wanted?" I say. "I don't recollect wanting this stuff at all."

"Silence on the line!" Sergeant Silas hisses, short-circuiting communications for the duration.

The duration turns out to be a test of everyone's endurance. The path to our plateau of choice is three miles of very steep gradient. The heat, which is so constant in these islands you can quickly forget you were ever comfortable, is more intense than anything we have encountered yet. Practically the only sound we hear is the full-body assault of marines up ahead chopping maniacally at the overgrowth with machetes. I can hear the effort that is going into it and I think it makes me sweat even more heavily.

This is where we can thank our lucky stars and lunatic training for all those months that got us in optimal condition. Because by the first mile, my camo is soaked through beyond saturation point. Sweat is running down my back, down my legs, into my boots like I'm filling them from a particularly fetid tap. If I was required to do anything more than propel myself forward and upward carrying my own fifty pounds of gear, I don't know if I could do it. My legs are telling me that the first mile was actually ten, because despite the best efforts of machete and man, the ground beneath us is a hacked-up hodgepodge of strappingly unchoppable vines, broad slippery leaves and shoots that have fallen on top of them, and mud underneath it all. The mud here is a whole new species to me, something like the consistency of axle grease laid down half a foot deep before you reach anything like a solid earth supporting it.

It is misery every step, and the sounds of tough, trained-up, maximum marines trying to muffle grunts and exhausted groans of effort is almost more painful than if we had to listen to people scream out through it all.

The only creatures so far seeming to hold up well are the flying insects, of which there are billions. I cannot go more than two steps without swatting at them, so I don't think about it after a while, I just go into auto-swat, windmilling rhythmically at the places on my neck and face and arms they seem to find most appetizing. The blackness is far, far too absolute to see these creatures, but some of them have to be big as bats from the sounds, and from the nips they're laying on me. Maybe they *are* bats. Only, sometimes I can't be sure if it's one of the bugs or one of the many lashing and gashing branches pressing into me from the tight fit of the corridor we are just about managing to cut through this great monstrous beast of a jungle.

I'm shredded to tatters, when suddenly I detect a change. It's a slight lifting of the density of the air, a faint sense of men indulging in the sweet sighs of release farther up the line. Ours is the third platoon in the column, and we can see the breathable world opening up gradually to us in the distance as one and another and another sweat-hog devil dog emerges onto the plateau of our dreams.

I hear the sound come out of me the moment I emerge from the hothouse misery. It's exactly the sound I would make when bursting up out of the water, after diving far too deep for my lungs' liking.

First thing we do is gather in squad-size groupings to pull ourselves together. The first thing I say when I am allowed to speak is addressed directly to Corporal Havlicek.

"How right do you have to be?"

"I did tell you, though," he says, forcing enough of a smile to be recognizable through his grimace.

"Yeah, but . . ." It becomes quickly apparent that even speaking will require pacing myself. "You're always right enough. Now you say something and it seems to be hyper-right, like God just wants to please you, personally."

"If that is the case," he says, "I'm going to have a word with God. Because I am not pleased."

"This jungle," Klecko says, slow and measured, "is the jungle that Vella's jungle wants to be when it grows up."

The game but underpowered laugh that ripples around our group is a saddening thing. The echo from a family of prairie dogs yipping at the bottom of an enormous canyon would sound just about like we do now.

We probably do a fair impression of the industrious little creatures again as we spend the next several hours constructing our marine-style den of necessities on our small patch of Choiseul high ground. Plateau dogs, you could call us, as we scurry around, digging holes, cutting paths, establishing lookout posts at the far seaward edges of our established perimeter. We get communications set up and all the vital equipment in place, the basics for getting us through till the morning comes and daylight brings a whole new bunch of necessities and objectives.

It is routine stuff and not backbreaking, but by the time we set up our bivouac and climb up for our first time into new hammocks strung between trees, we are aching for that little bit of relief under that new Choiseul moon looking right at us.

At first light we get into motion finishing our camp off to make it a proper command post for our operations. But we've barely got the sleep out of our eyes when a Japanese bomber comes barreling in from the north, heading right for us. It was unlikely that we could have made this landing and gotten settled in so easily without the enemy knowing we were around somewhere. It is still a Japanese-held island, a fact we should remember as we do our chores.

For a minute or two we are all suspended, watching the plane come on, growing bigger, louder, showing us his fat belly full of doom. Then, he releases his load, two five-hundred-pound bombs that we watch roll and plummet and then *BOOM*, one falls right into the water, the very spot where we disembarked last night. Then the second lands *BOOM* just beyond the waterline, thumping into the beach below us, throwing sand plumes up almost as high as we are now. The impact shakes the whole hill and makes the ground under us tremble as if we were standing on top of a rickety, condemned building.

"Well, they know where we've already been," Klecko says.

"Let's get back to work, men," Sergeant Silas says, "before they catch up to where we *are*."

That sounds like a reasonable idea to me. And to everyone else, I guess, as each man goes double-time on his task with new energy and determination. We look like a professional building site, or the Navy's in-house engineering team, the Seabees, as we get in gear.

"Nothing like a fresh-brewed bombing raid first thing in the morning to get a guy motivated, eh, fellas?" Bryant says. Nobody answers, but you don't need responses when you are as right as that.

Almost as soon as we have a fully assembled command center, officer types start commanding and just like that, our whole demolition platoon, which is us and two more ten-man squads configured just like ours, has got marching orders. And so do three rifle platoons of fifteen men each, including five mortars. We're descending methodically down the eastern side of the hill on a patrol to discover where the enemy might be hunkered down. We know where their major encampments are, but everyone figures they're going to be found in a bunch of other places as well. We're trying to root them out of any place that lies between the plateau and our destination, which is the back side of the barge station at Sangigai. The plan is to attack the station from two directions. Another group will approach it head-on by returning to our landing area and marching up the beach to the northeast. We will be going the more deceptive — and far more challenging — inland route to shock them by emerging right behind their position.

That is, once we have cleared the route. We say "cleared" a lot, which mostly means killing everybody you find in an area you don't want them to be in.

"All right, now it's starting to feel real," my trusted lead machine gunner whispers. Good thing his assistant is always close enough to hear his hushed words.

"Very, very real," I whisper back, with a little extra huff-puff to my nervous voice. "So real, in fact, we need to stop talking at all."

"Got it."

"Shut up."

The sweat is back again. The heat of the daytime is well beyond even last night's steaminess, and it feels like instead of cooling us, the jungle just seals the humid heat inside and then works with the death-ray sunshine to magnify it times a thousand. I am reminded again of Klecko's ant comparison for us, and I am filled with remorse for every last ant I burned with a magnifying glass as a kid.

The flying insects have returned as well, only this time it feels too dangerous to even smack them for fear of attracting Japanese stingers that won't feel better with a little calamine lotion rubbed into them.

It does not feel as if I have seventy-five of my closest heavily armed friends by my side as we creep along essentially the same route. Because of the permanent dusk under the tree cover and the thickness of the growth down here and the requirement for silence, it feels for the most part shockingly lonely in this place we're creeping through. Our famous esprit de corps is a very real thing, but it can't do anything for us right now.

Klecko is the only marine I can see at all times. And of course he is the one I would choose if I had the choice to make, but still I wouldn't mind seeing a whole bunch of them right about now.

Suddenly, I see him hold up a hand for me to freeze and that is what I do while holding up my hand for the man behind. Sweat and insects now slither up and down and across my skin from scalp to ankles and everywhere in between as I play statues in a forest that surely does not want me here. I hold my discipline, have faith in my training, and remain hawkeyed. I survey all around me and resist the urge to stare at Klecko's hand until I can make it go down with my desperate willpower.

His hand remains up there so long I swear I can feel my hair falling out of my head, one strand at a time. *Plink*. There goes one. *Plink*. There goes one.

Klecko's hand goes down, releasing us to move. My hand goes down. We move.

Here and there, in no real pattern, clearings open up like tiny dream settlements in the middle of density that is nothing short of a freakish deformity of nature, surely never meant to be like this. As we pass through one now I get a boyish, thrilled relief at the sight of Corporal Havlicek leading Klecko at the head of our column. Then he's gone just as quickly as if we have been wandering lost and alone the whole time and the corporal was a phantom.

Because of the relentlessly contrary nature of the terrain, we are not in a true USMC formation at all.

Theoretically, each platoon should be breaking down into its individual formation, like a wedge, or a V, with the squads falling in within that.

But officers on this patrol recognized immediately that nothing complicated was going to hold in such an unyielding jungle, where it's hard enough for one man to walk in a straight line for long. So we are still under the originally planned command structure, but the reality is that we are functioning as a great mass of individual five-man fire teams flowing down one big hillside.

And the fire teams are straight lines. And because everybody apparently loves to have machine gunners at the front of something completely unknown and unquestionably dangerous, Klecko and I are basically at the leading edge of one column of teams. Somewhere nearby, Bryant and Westphal are following behind Sergeant Silas at the spearhead of another.

We pass through another clearing and I breathe as much of it as I can before stepping out of it again.

Then another one is in front of us much more quickly than I'd expect. No complaints on that from me. At this stage, two relatively airy clearings within sight of one another deserves appreciation, if not celebration.

Celebration then ends abruptly. Havlicek starts waving his arm madly down, down, down, then Klecko waves down, down, down before diving for the ground. I motion down, down, down and then immediately show Heads and Tails behind me just what it means. I hit the ground hard, like I'm trying to crash right through it and maybe come up the complete other side to emerge in Sandusky, Ohio. Or maybe even better, the pitcher's mound of the ballpark in Centreville, Maryland. Home of both the Red Sox entry in the Class D Eastern Shore League, and my dreams for the future.

I don't break through to anywhere, though. Instead, I slither along on my belly just like in so many training drills. In a few seconds, Klecko and me are flanking Havlicek as the three of us crouch behind the fat old husk of a long-fallen tree. Havlicek is talking low into his radio.

"Yes, we see them. Looks like they're transferring ammo from the barges into a secret dump underground. Right. You're in range. Doing it now. In ninety . . ."

He's leaning harder into the fallen trunk, as if his plan is to roll ten tons of rotting wood to flatten the patrol of ten Japanese soldiers.

"Line them up," he says, and this is business and no fooling.

Klecko and I have our machine guns up and we use the top of the trunk for steadying. It's still an effort for me to keep from trembling the enemies right out of my sights. But I remember to be a marine about it, and I get it controlled.

"Bigger than I thought they'd be," Klecko says.

"That's 'cause you're looking at imperial marines and not Army. And when I count you down from five seconds you are going to set your sights on one individual big imperial marine and you are going to fire that weapon at only that man and keep on firing until he is dead. Then, move on. You understand, both of you?"

"Yes," we both do, and we both say.

Other teams are locking in from around our position.

RattaTattaTattaTattaTattaTatta

It's a barrage of machine-gun and rifle fire, but it's coming from the wrong guys. Something pulled their attention, and the Japanese marines are pouring heavy-caliber heat into one of the teams thirty yards up the line from us.

"Fire, fire, fire!" Havlicek barks in the loudest voice we have heard since leaving Vella Lavella.

Already locked on target, Klecko and I join the fight with a series of blasts from the Reisings, and our rounds look to be shooting as straight as any man's weapon in any man's army could ever do.

Two Japanese machine gunners wheel in our direction and we go from short blasts to all-out unbroken streams of bullets aiming at those machine gunners as their ammo whistles and pings the air, the trees around us, very close. Several shots make mini tremors in the big old tree trunk right in front of us. The trunk has now saved my life at least a dozen times as these guys' aim keeps getting better, death keeps coming closer, and we are just not having it. I feel myself leaning in, flopping over the top of the trunk in an effort to get a better read on my man and I have it, perfect, and as we empty round after round in the Japanese direction I watch my man, watch him go down, watch him fall, his gun dropping harmlessly out of his grip before he pitches forward and I follow through locked on to him until his face bounces off the ground, settles there forever, and my steaming overheated machine goes *clickety clickety clickety* as the bullets run out well before I do.

I turn toward Klecko on my left, find him likewise overextended on top of the tree trunk and firing *clickety clickety clickety* at the seven Japanese corpses spread across the ground and the three who have retreated beyond our range but not beyond our sights or our memories.

"I think killing is starting to become a habit for me," I say, dismayed to hear the words and the lack of human feeling behind them.

"Did you pick the one far left?" Zack says as we push ourselves off the log and stand up.

"Yeah. Same one for you? What am I saying? Of course we picked the same. Bet we do that a hundred times out of a hundred, whatcha think?"

"What I think is that I think we both killed him, is what I think. So I figure I've lightened the burden on your soul by one half of one enemy kill."

"Thanks," I say, just before Corporal Havlicek seizes control of the subject.

"*Now*, marines. No time for being triumphant. Move out, all of you. Back up the road, pronto. Heading back to base immediately. We are no secret to anybody now, and if we don't fight fleet and we don't fight clever the enemy is going to put two and two *thousand* together and realize we are not a full division and that they have a five-to-one manpower advantage. I don't think we want that," he says, waving guys on up the hill like a scowling and very serious traffic cop. When

Klecko passes him, and then I do, with Heads and Tails jumping into line behind me like they're hopping a bus, only then does the good corporal start trekking himself. He marches briskly alongside the fire team, overtakes us, and slips into his rightful slot as our leader.

Darkness falls on Choiseul rapidly and absolutely, the way a big imperial marine pitches himself forward and down. Cold and senseless and complete. He planted his dead face into the island's brutal, merciless ground because this was the place he chose to die.

I settle into my swaying hammock, under my comforting mosquito netting and that same moon, too. Today was real war, and tomorrow is already planned to be real, realer still, war. I love the way a hammock sways, barely perceptible but completely altering the life it's supporting, suspending it three feet above that rotten, cruel ground.

Zachary Klecko's hammock is tied at one end to the same tree as mine. We sleep head to head, or head-tree-head, but close enough to communicate and still keep to a modified whisper.

"Zack," I say after ten swaying minutes spent with more of my thoughts than I would consider optimal.

"Yeah?"

"Other guys could have shot him."

He waits a beat or two, a sway or three.

"Nope," he says confidently.

"But what if they did? What if one or maybe more than one other guy was laying into our guy at the same time we were?"

"I'm not sharing. I think I'm already being generous enough by giving you benefit of the doubt and a fifty percent share. I'm not diluting the shares any further, especially since I hit him with at least twenty shots myself and that would be indisputably dead by any rational measure."

I sigh, to send a message to the big-head gunner officially rated as Expert marksman. "I'm going to ignore the parts of that where I'm not agreeing with you but I'm not rising to the bait, either. I never chased a ball outside the strike zone before and I'm not doing it now."

"Also, with the positioning of both sides, the angle of our firing line and all that, the shortest distance between dead enemy, far left, and anything coming from our side, was from his chest to my gun. So all my rounds would have got to him before all of anybody else's."

"Have you actually been preparing this?"

"I'm only trying to relieve your aching conscience."

"Yeah, well I'd prefer you just keep your hands off of my conscience. I can handle it just fine."

"If you say so."

"I just did. But I can do it again if you like."

He fake-yawns the conversation toward closing time. "No, that'll be all, private," he adds, in a tired voice that does not contain the fakery.

I have to open it up again, just a crack.

"So, what if other guys hit him, and we simply missed him every time. It does happen."

"No, Nicholas, it does not. I think you got malaria. Go to sleep."

Sleep, yes. He is technically my immediate supervisor, so I must obey a direct order.

And I do, directly; for the second night running I get the sound, deeply restful night of unconsciousness that I never got on Vella Lavella. Or anywhere else, come to think of it.

It's a strange and unsettling sensation, and I've only felt it once before. My first season in pro baseball, lowest rung league on the climb up to the bigs. I got hit right in the temple with a huge, blistering beanball. For two weeks I was seeing three of everything, and I also kept getting lost, even in my own neighborhood.

That's a little like how this feels. We're on this mission, to create a mighty racket, hit and run and disappear and blow stuff up and shoot Japanese fighters. All as just a diversion, to fool them into sending troops here from Bougainville — which is the real target for the invasion. If we succeed and live, our big prize is we get to join those boys over there at the genuine actual invasion.

So, we are expected to make big impressions here, to get them to try and come after us. To kill us.

But at the same time, we are slithering and tiptoeing and shushing each other because — oh, right, by the way — we don't really want to get killed.

It all feels slightly as if we're getting mentally messed up by our own side. Can a marine ever wobble in this kind of way? Is it permissible? I would bet not.

I think it would take an awfully long time to really fully understand the military. More time than I will ever have. That's why the Marines' structure at the lowest level — that would be my level — has its own built-in, brilliant purpose: Take care of your own patch, your own function, your own task, your duties to your comrades within your own perimeter, and everything will work out. Trying to raise your head and figure out all the bigger pictures puts that head in too much jeopardy.

My patch, my function, my buddies. Right.

A buddy and a buddy, both fiercely committed to never getting separated, is a beautiful thing. What happens, though, if a buddy starts to worry about getting separated from himself?

This marine is going to fiercely commit to not finding out.

There is one element of USMC functioning at the higher levels that I do find reassuringly reliable.

That element is The Brute. The commander of the whole operation, he has personally led our section, Company F, on our mission to cause maximum mayhem and destruction to both the barge station at Sangigai, and the Japanese sense of security on Choiseul Island. While the two other companies set out to execute their business elsewhere on the island, F Company is marching on the east side of Sangigai, timed to coincide with E Company hitting them from the west for a crusher maneuver that should be brutal. We stomp along to the destination with a certainty that ignores how dangerously outnumbered we are in this place. It's a certainty that's surely filtering down from our leader, The Brute himself.

I don't think that man has had one uncertain moment his whole life.

We are approaching our destination, maybe a quarter mile east along the beach that we can just now see. My heartbeat is picking up as the action comes nearer and realer and it's evident in the rest of the guys as well. Heads start bobbing a little more emphatically, legs start bouncing that much higher as the nerves and adrenaline of a coming fight turn men into show horses at around this stage.

We are about to take on the more raucous side of our split-personality profile, which is a welcome change. It's the softly-softly, creepy silence of the jungle maneuvers that'll make you nuts, way before the brawling-mauling danger that comes with wide-open warfare will.

I'm certain every single marine feels the same way. Our Dr. Gentle / Mr. Mental conflict would only ever have one victor. And he is no doctor.

We come to the patch where the jungle density gradually lets up a bit the closer you get to the beach. The extra oxygen will come in handy for our impending engagement with the enemy.

The festive atmosphere is supercharged by the knowledge that our ground forces are going to be aided by an air bombardment coming from Vella Lavella.

Shuuuuush-poom!

That, however, is not an American bomb, but a Japanese rocket-propelled grenade. It scorches the air as it parts the company right down the middle and sails into the trees behind us.

"Cover!" the commander yells and platoon and squad leaders up and down the line echo the command. "And: *Fire!*" The Brute roars. He must have some big thick roots running from his small self, down through the ground and hundreds of feet into earth, to sound as giant as that.

Giant sounds are now the order of the day. These woods are completely jammed up with rifle fire, grenades, and the screams of angry men mixed with the screams of men who suddenly find themselves hit, ventilated and dying. I am crouched behind one side of a fat banyan tree, with my buddy and machine gun partner on the other side.

"Plenty for everyone today," Klecko yells out over the sound of his Reising picking off their fair share.

"Nah," I call back. "These ones are all mine."

He laughs a howl of a wild laugh, made more so by the *ratatat-ratatat-ratatattat* music backing it up.

It was a bold assertion on my part, worthy of a laugh, since there are probably one hundred and fifty Japanese fighters I'd need to be killing. Fighters who, once again, were not supposed to be here. What is it with these guys and being where they're not expected?

The smells are combining again. The singular mud and sweat and greenery scent that is already planted in my head from this place is expanding. It's gaining layers and powers as smoke from a huge range of weapons and gun oils swirls and blends in. The most common Japanese rifles are famous for their heavy, stinky coating of grease, and it's nasty. Famous also for shooting Americans dead from every sneaky and crafty angle imaginable. The sudden overpowering whiff of blood comes up and reminds me of that fact. Somebody not more than twenty yards down the fire line to my right is hit and falls screaming into the bloody mud in front of him. Dozens of Japanese go down, and while I did not dare look over at my brother marine, I get a clear look at each one of my enemies as he leaves the fight for now and for good.

This is every bit the craziness of the firefight, all at

once. It's so intense I don't even hear the roaring engines of the bombers from Vella now reaching the island and its several targets.

Bu-hoom. Bu-hoom bu-hoom bu-hoom-bu-hoom.

It is more shocking and frightening than I'd expected as the bombs pound the nearby barge base. It stuns me briefly and I stop shooting and start staring.

"Nardini, fire that weapon!" Havlicek screams, aware the very second I have gone off plan. "Fire!"

So I fire. Everybody fires, and fires and fires and fires, the whole Mr. Mental company fires blissfully away.

We have our prize.

Because we did our job and then some on Choiseul, we are now moving on to Bougainville. We executed Operation Blissful better than probably anybody expected, and executed an estimated hundred and forty or so unlucky Japanese fighters in the bargain. We hit them in every spot, with every shot. We were like the school-yard jerk, going around picking fights, getting our licks in, then running away again to pick another fight just a few yards away. We did that over and over again. It was tiring work, but satisfying.

"I don't feel like I need to keep count anymore," I say as the Higgins boats speed us away from Choiseul mostly unscathed. About a dozen wounded. Nine of our guys killed. Nobody I knew really well, though.

"No," Klecko says with a bit of surprise. "No, you're right. I was feeling exactly the same just now. No need. No point after a point, I guess."

"I guess," I say.

CHAPTER EIGHT

The Dead of Night

The confidence we brought to the fights throughout Blissful is even higher by the time we move on. It is a step up, a big challenge compared to our previous island and our operations there. But we are learning our craft quickly, and the men who land on Bougainville are smarter, tougher, more daring, and more prepared than they were before.

"How does it keep happening?" Klecko says with frothing frustration.

We're finishing off digging out our second foxhole in only our second night on the island.

"Which *it* is that, Zack?"

"The it that makes each island up on the chain at least twice as nasty as the last one?"

We both stop digging, but continue sweating and swatting. The bugs here are the drill instructors that taught the bugs we met before.

I shrug, which I find I'm doing a lot more of lately. "Good planning and resource management?"

"Thanks for that," he says.

Klecko and I jump, backward and nearly out of our skins, when a breathy, angry voice behind us practically bites my ear. "If you two do not shut up this minute," Sergeant Silas says, "I will shoot you myself in my duty of care to all the other men who should not have to get killed by the enemies you will bring to our foxholes."

We are trying to get smoothly to our feet after stumbling around like a couple of lousy comics from the initial shock. It's quite dark, but still easy to see our very serious squad leader brandishing a very serious pistol in his hand.

"I am serious," Silas assures us in low, slow syllables.

"Yeah, we get that," Klecko says. "Sorry, sergeant. Won't happen again."

With that skirmish over, we settle in and get comfy for the night in our hole.

This is as far as you could get from our hammocks of bliss, the memory of which is already slipping fast and far away from us.

My buddy, for his part, doesn't struggle in the same way I do. He nestles down on his side, facing me so we both are watching the other man's back. He silently gives me his disapproving "not this again" scowl.

I match his scowl with my "not a chance" head shake and we both understand that I will never sleep in a foxhole even if I am stuck in one for a hundred nights. Bougainville is already, even outside of this hole in the ground, the creepiest and most unsettling place I have been in my life. There are Japanese military and civilians absolutely everywhere. But mostly underground, in caves and spider holes that we've been told are connected up with miles and miles of tunnels they've been preparing just for this occasion for years. That alone would disturb your sleep. But they also have a real fondness for doing most of their dirty work at night. They slip aboveground and then move about this strangely forested place like smoke. They know all the things we never will about the terrain here, and when they are not trying to cozy on down into your foxhole and slit your throat, they are lying low just a few feet off in the dark, whispering Japanese jerk stuff that a guy does not need translated in order to wet his pants over.

When the thing that passes for daylight here finally arrives, I take it like a starter's pistol and bound up out of that moist and foul grave we dug ourselves. Two nights of no sleep has me gaining new edges every hour, and this is just the beginning.

I go to the next hole over, about twenty feet off, just to make the proper contact with somebody on the good guys' team.

I'm within eight feet of the foxhole before I even register what I'm seeing. The two demolition guys, Chaney and Satchel, the ones I didn't really know that well anyway. They have got new, gaping and oozing mouths on them, right across their throats. Their heads are pivoted all the way back, in case we missed what had happened. They are covered in flying whatevers already and an early-bird rat is catching the worm out of Chaney's gullet.

All of that just twenty feet from where my buddy and I spent the long, quiet night.

Payback is assured. Especially among a population like this, armed, trained, and willing. Especially in a place like this, at a time like this. Where rules and laws, rights and wrongs are defined and redefined constantly, even daily, and always by the side with the higher firepower and outrage.

We have a patrol lined up already and we take to the trail faster than any unit normally moves first thing in the morning. Like Choiseul, only worse, the heat and the savage biting insects are working on us before we get very far, but it sure doesn't deter Klecko, who is setting the pace and making it tough for me to keep up. We are out in a four-man fire team of me and Klecko, Heads and Tails. The demolition men are more and more involved the farther we move up the Slot through the Solomons chain. Each island is, again, more inhospitable and hard to navigate than the previous one, but also, each one is more riddled with the famous Japanese honeycomb of caves. People hide so deep you can't see. Then sometimes they escape out an exit fifty yards away and it's real frustrating. But the big thing is, there is no way of telling anything once we find a hole in the ground. A cave could hold three fighters or twelve women and children. There could be an escape route or often nothing but a hole in the ground where they are all backed to the wall. Nearly impossible to tell one from another, but the last thing you want to do is stand over a cave with your big mug staring in waiting for your whole fat head to be blown away.

So, what you do want is demo guys, for one.

"There," Klecko barks, and Tails throws himself — bravely or nuttily is debatable — across the ground in the direction of a well-concealed hole where a thick rotting tree trunk is hollowed out and placed perfectly over the hole like a large wooden coffin lid.

"Get up, get up here! Right now, right now, right now or I'm gonna kill ya right where you are ya bunch of cave hole cowards."

I have seen nothing to compare with the energy, the volume, the raw violence Tails is radiating right now in pure Grade-A USMC loyalty to his fallen comrades in the demolition brotherhood.

"Okay then, guess what?" he screams down the hole even louder. "You're coming out anyway!" He's taken a thing off his belt, a sort of canister with a long fuse coming out of the top. I have never seen any explosive that looked like it, but most likely neither has anyone other than Heads and Tails.

But he doesn't light the fuse. He yanks it straight out, like we once did with our parachute rip cords. He throws the device down the hole.

I keep a constant lookout over the perimeter, pointing my machine gun in a wide arc over my half of the patch, while Klecko is supposed to be doing the same. "Keep watch, Zachary," I snap, but he is fixated on the hole and what is happening in it.

There is banging, hissing, sizzling. Sparks shoot and shine inside the cave and then up about ten feet above the ground. Smoke follows that, a deep green soupy smoke that is already burning my eyes and nostrils from twenty feet, so I can only imagine what it's doing to the unfortunates down inside with the thing.

It is like a whole entire fireworks show, though contained in a smaller space than would be recommended for any show.

And, as we notice when a man comes flailing and screaming out of the hole, these fireworks would be unlikely to get a license to pop anywhere but in a military setting. The enemy soldier leaps and thrashes like he's a marlin and Tails has hooked and hauled him in. It is an impressive exit, the guy shooting up like he was rocket propelled. Then he hits the ground with a crunch everybody can hear because he is too agonized by every other thing to worry about breaking his fall with his hands.

As he writhes on the ground, we inch closer and watch as the skin covering his hands, face, and neck puckers and boils like pea soup overheating on a stove. The man is screaming; his eyes look like they want to propel themselves right out of his bony skull and come over to join our side. They are wild, the eyes, bleach white and blood-vessel orange. There are jagged shards of metal protruding in a staggered line running from the soft skin in front of his ear, over his collarbone, and under his arm.

The explosive Tails just introduced to the world — but mostly to one nearly-former inhabitant of it — has got everything in it, from phosphorus smoke, to some kind of acid, and even shrapnel. It's a nasty little masterpiece, is what it is.

"Nice," Heads says, walking up beside Tails and putting a hand on his shoulder. The two of them stand close to the man, who is in more agony every second, and watch as if it is a field experiment.

The Japanese fighter, on his knees, turns upward to attempt to see the guys. He toggles his head side to side trying to catch the sound since his eyes are missing in action. He is slapping and rubbing and patting every burning part of himself, which is every part, and he bends and howls and comes back up and his horrible melting hands and his bent, begging posture and his crying, crying shattered glass voice are all unmistakably begging the men to kill him quickly and mercifully.

Heads acts like a stupid tourist who doesn't know the local language.

"What? Yes, I agree, you shouldn't slit a man's throat while he's sleeping. It is shameful, yes it is."

The man is screaming as hard as he can, but it's as if there is a hand somewhere gradually turning his volume dial down. His body seems to be shrinking, dissolving under the caustic fury of the chemical device and of its maker.

I look over to Klecko, who has suddenly rediscovered his dedication to scanning the perimeter in the opposite direction. I look more closely at our scientists, as the man's screams don't sound like they will be reaching any conclusions any time soon.

I found them, for crying out loud. I wanted to slice every last Japanese throat on the island not long ago. But not long ago is getting longer ago every second, and whoever this melting, crying man is, he is not going anywhere as far as I can tell. My flesh starts doing something in sympathy for this creature, because there is nothing but creature there now, whoever he might have been once — teacher, bus driver, fisherman. My ears are trying to retract while I stand here with a machine gun and bounce up high on the balls of my feet involuntarily.

The man's wailing is broken only by a wild ruckus not thirty yards along this same trail. Our new comrades, secret weapons, and man's best friends are barking and howling their vicious pointed faces off. Meaning the K-9 Corps has cornered enemy fighters in hidey-holes. A whole big swarm of them, from the sound of things.

Heads and Tails run down the trail, thoughtless and quick as rabbits. They're rabid with grief and fear and there's nothing for it I guess but the reflex of revenge. And explosions, which I would imagine could be a comfort to certain explosive types. Unwise to go off like that, really, dangerous and foolhardy, but I've never found geniuses to be very bright, anyway.

The man's screaming is still full-throated, but it sounds like a runty lamb who's too frail to survive and too simple to understand. The hands around her tiny throat are only there squeezing her with kindness, choking her out of compassion, out of her misery. "Baahh," the lamb man says, from his back, from the ground. "Baaahh."

I am staring as I walk toward the little lamb man, staring at my partner, who is duty bound to watch the perimeter for people like us except Japanese.

"Baaahh," he says, smaller than any lamb, surely. As I look at Klecko's broad back I *rattatattatta* fire one burst of machine-gun rounds into that little head, and thank God, the sound ceases.

I start making my way up the path toward the

Doberman pinschers. What luck, our newest colleagues working practically right next door.

"You coming?" I say without looking back.

"Not so loud, will ya?" he says, already right behind me.

It's night again. We're in a foxhole again. I have my knife in my hand and my buddy's head resting on my lap. The knife is because unless I'm manning my gun, I do not spend one second in a foxhole anymore without my knife in my hand. An hour ago I stabbed a snake right through its head. The foxhole is shallow because if we dig more than three feet down the ooze starts rising. It oozed us in our first hole of the evening, coming up slowly and the same temperature as the rotten air here, so we didn't even notice we were getting oozed until it became visible making its way up our legs. I flew up out of the hole as if a land mine had blasted me. Threw off every stitch of clothing on me, as I felt the slime clinging to me, seeping into my skin, making me itch like a filthy rat dog. Klecko had it on him, too, of course, but he undressed much more calmly. He was clearly not suffering like I was, and he had the bonus of enjoying my dancing dirtball act to take his mind off his own discomfort. It may sound strange, but having him there laughing at me was swell. Kept me from going a lot loonier, and this is how it's been. We seem to have a rhythm going where one of us goes into one kind of fit or another while his buddy supervises. It's a system that somehow devised itself, just like our night-talking has evolved. It naturally tuned down lower, lower, because we could not survive without the contact, no way, no way. It's a magic kind of thing we got now, a private buddyspeak like dog whistles that nobody else can hear, combined with tiny little tongue clickings that came out of nowhere, but we knew and know and that's just us.

And the reason his big head is resting in my lap is that it's a thing we saw Sergeant Silas doing with his bunkmate, Havlicek. "It's a thing this guy and his gang brought back from Guadalcanal," the sergeant told us. "Better comfort, better sleep, better watching out for trouble when you alternate positions every couple of hours."

Turned out to be good advice, but I won't be sleeping, so I just do all the upright shifts myself. Works dandy for us, though, because he gets solid rest for the both of us and I can keep talking through the night. I like that, talking to him, whether he's awake or not. The day on Bougainville had been a relentless, head-shattering noise of bomber planes attacking Japanese positions in their pillbox fortifications. They are only made of coconut logs, coral, and mud, but they seem all but indestructible. The bombers bomb, the enemy responds with antiaircraft shells, our guys respond with mortar fire up into positions near the top of the hill, and all day both sides shoot and shoot and shoot, throw grenades at each other, and shoot some more.

Then night comes down, curtain drops, show's over kids, everybody shush now.

There is so much shush here. So much shush in the night I pray somebody will set off rockets, machine gun the sky, anything, because my ears are screaming and I can hear every rivulet of sweat babbling the whole way down the length of me.

I stabbed the snake when it was right at my eye level. It remained pinned there while I watched it up close, dying and dead by my hand, and that was the only cheerful moment of my day. Lifted my spirits up right through all three layers of tree canopy above us. The only reason I don't have the snake pinned any-more is my arm started to cramp after twenty minutes and my arm was never coming back to me without that knife grasped tightly in its fist. Snake is still there, though, with its gaping head, so at least that's something.

"This is the worst, Zack," I say in click-whisper. He's been out for a while, so I don't expect an answer.

"It is," he says anyway. "Those last two islands were luxury holidays compared to this."

"No, I mean the worst, of everything, everywhere, ever."

"Ah c'mon. It's a lot like camping out, when we were in the scouts when we were kids. Remember?"

"I remember the scouts, but I don't remember what you remember, apparently."

"Come on, sure you do. Same as this, except tents instead of stinkholes and maybe a little less stabbiness and . . . ah, there ya go. Head-stabbed snakes and everything. You do that?"

"Yeah," I say, perking up with tiny jolts of pride and insect stinging.

"See, you do remember."

I can feel when his body goes to sleep, and it goes just like that.

"It's been raining nonstop since we've been here."

He wakes just like that. "Not nonstop."

"Nonstop."

"It's not raining now," he says.

I look straight up for a second. He's right. A second later, it starts raining.

"Yes, it is," I say, with the triumphant sense of a man who can make it rain.

"Okay, it is. But it's not been nonstop. It stops all the time. It just starts up again right away, that's all."

"Fine. Go back to sleep."

There is no debate about whether it's raining or not now. It is coming down so hard and relentless today, it sounds more like machine-gun fire than machine-gun fire does.

With the squad down to eight men it's a fairly easy rotation of groups of four, with each group taking one demolition guy and one boss type. The two machine-gunner teams do not get broken up ever, and so Klecko and I are more or less the planet around which all the smaller moons revolve. As it should be.

"Guadalcanal," Corporal Havlicek says as we slog up one of the few actual trails the Seabees have managed to cut through this monstrous place. It is a mixed blessing, however, as without any of that ground cover holding it together, the ground is one foot deep of pure rancid muck. I have not seen my feet or lower legs in an hour.

"You mean the rain?" I ask, half turning to speak low to him as he's walking behind me. The machine gunners lead today, with Klecko ahead of Tails just the other side of the road from us.

"Eyes front," Havlicek says. We splash forward toward our objective, another fifteen minutes up the way. "The rain, yeah. More the stench. There's more rotting man in this air than any place I've been since the 'Canal."

"Sorry I missed it," I say.

"Careful of rash judgments, private. You might not have missed it yet."

That's a cheery thought to perk up my day. That, and the reminder of the rash that's begun to spread, purple ivy blooming its way up my whole lower half.

We get to the spot. And we have drilled this over and over to the point where there's no communication necessary. The four of us fan right out, off the side of the road and down sixty long yards that is not the muck trough that the road is, but plenty bad in its own way. Every silent, gentle step I take over the slime-slippy, viney hillside releases mushroom clouds of insects that are in my mouth before I can close it, in my ears and nostrils after I do. They are swarming, in me and over me, and I want to vomit, and cough, spit and slap them until I am blue in the face.

But I am an American marine. And this is my gun.

Never loved those soldier's creeds we were required to memorize. But the words give me something to cling to as I do absolutely nothing about the filthy invaders all over me and my comrades.

We stalk, like panthers. That's what we do.

The target is one of the legendary pillboxes the Japanese are so successful with. A recon working way down low on the hill identified it up here, ideally placed for attacking ground troops below and low-flying aircraft above. Depending on their armaments, even landing craft would not be safe from these well-dug gun nests. The hill itself has been their protector, as the shelter is completely invisible from the relatively well-traveled road above, and we have been waiting for these lovely flood conditions for our chance, when they would be least suspicious of a descent and not too enthusiastic about leaving the house so often to check.

We are in place. I am set up with my machine gun wide left, with Klecko wide right. We are lying down, training our sights on the front edges of the structure where anyone coming for us would first appear, around the corner from the lone front opening. We are at a substantial downhill angle, and the miserable bugwater, the stinking runoff of a thousand rotting corpses, is cascading right down the hill and up my legs and into my shirt and this time there is no option. I vomit up today's thousand calories of K and C rations, spreading it all out just in front of me while I remain steadfast, my eye never moving from the sight.

Corporal Havlicek takes a position right in the middle, taking aim with his Johnson semiautomatic rifle that Klecko and I would trade both our Reisings for.

Tails ducks and slides and weaves his way down to the pillbox, fast and fearless. I'm right now glad we won him today in the now-routine coin toss that decides which team gets him or Heads. I came up with the process.

He is nearly there and I am terrified for him. No one has peeked around either corner by the time he is within ten yards. He was game, sure, and excited when we went over the plan, with the drawing of the opening he had to make. There will be as many as ten Japanese in the box at any one time and with no action down there now we can't even estimate from their gunfire. Once he hits the corner he is to whip himself halfway around the front of it and in the same motion hurl his specially constructed package of TNT, grenades, and assorted smaller goodies that are designed to go boom with just enough time to unwhip himself from that opening but not enough time to let anyone else out after him.

That is the plan, anyway.

But the plan is blown to smithereens when a Japanese lookout steps around the corner at the very moment Tails has crawled up to the ground right in front of him.

Tails freezes. The startled lookout fumbles with his gun.

And the crack of a single round from the Johnson semiautomatic shakes the jungle floor beneath us as the lookout's head snaps back and he follows it, hurtling backward down the hill.

Tails has scrambled to his mark before the dead man has even stopped his downhill run. He slings his package into the box at feet level, then executes his own expert sideways barrel roll rightward and away from the scene so fast I think he may have some wheel in his bloodline somewhere.

Paww-waaw-waaw-waaaaaaw

The many different explosions go off in rapid succession, ending with a colossal *bhoooooommm* that blows a fat column of black smoke and fire and a geyser of human body parts including one head I can see so clearly that it spooks me into shouting as I look away from the clear, clear, clear toothy bloody grin he directs straight at me. When I turn back, the carnage and destruction is magnificent, but still comes off as the second most thrilling sight on this hill at this moment.

Tails's grin is a whole different thing but just as evident as he appears, run-crawling back up with the *aid* of this awful jungle. He scales the hill like a spider monkey and reaches the road at a clip, ahead of us all.

"Maintain discipline, marines," Havlicek tells us for the second time within ten minutes. "It's still a long road back."

He is as right as he always is. But it's hard not to bounce a bit more with our steps, to grin back and forth with our fantastic demolition man over our fantastic execution. It doesn't work so beautifully every day. Even when we are defeating the Japanese, pushing them back, getting jobs done, killing and not being killed, there are so many difficulties and setbacks and horrors, it can be easy to feel that winning doesn't feel much like winning.

This feeling, here, is rare, and the rush of it is as tough to fight off as some of the most fanatical Japanese fighters.

But that's what we have to do, because we are marines, professional fighting men, and discipline is the very minimum a squad leader can ask. There will be time to savor later, and we sure will.

The rain does its part to dampen spirits, and by the one-hour mark back along the main muck road we are very grim and serious fellows once more. My legs are getting heavy after all the marching and all the fluid I'm absorbing through the sores on my skin, the permanent underwater pollution of my desperate feet in these boots. I feel as if my burning skin should be causing steam to rise off my forehead when the raindrops pummel it. Then I remember: it rains hot water on Bougainville, the same temperature as me.

"Man down, to your right, Klecko," Havlicek snaps, and we all turn.

It is a fresh-killed Japanese rifleman. We stop, in our two-by-two formation, as Klecko walks off the side of the road to look.

"Proceed with extreme caution," the corporal says, and those are enough words to recall all the images we've been given of play-dead Japanese popping up and knifing a casual strolling American chump in the brain, by way of the soft tissue under the chin and the harder stuff at the roof of the mouth. Klecko stops abruptly five feet away from the rifleman, as if he heard my thought and froze. Turns out it's the opposite, and high spirits have returned to get the better of him.

"This should be cautious enough, then," he says, and lays into the body with a stream of automatic fire that would have killed this one and five more.

When Klecko turns and walks back our way, he is pleased and Corporal Havlicek is livid.

"You should have used —"

Bang-ping! Bang. B-b-b-b-bbang.

Snipers are on us, from well off the other side of the road.

"Down!" Havlicek barks, and everybody throws right down into the semisolid, putrid road. The two shooters are in trees one hundred yards straight ahead. I am again lying in complete muck as I take position, elbows down below the stuff, chin just dipping into it. I see both muzzle flashes as they continue to fire at us. The bang, the whistle, the plunk of one round hitting the muck a foot from my head is more stimulation than I need.

"Fire when you see your shots, men," Havlicek says just before they both open up again with semiautomatics and multiple muzzle flashes. The air whistles and the muck goes plunk as the Expert and the Sharpshooter level their barrels, train their sights, and send round after round straight up to the targets and the corporal's semiautomatic fills in any gaps and we fire and fire until we've emptied everything. We have to reload but we listen, listen for it, and there is nothing. Gorgeous nothing.

I do not take anything for granted and I don't take my eyes off those two killer bird nests in the distance. I load another cartridge in my gun and prepare for what tricky whatevers may still be to come. While I am lowering myself once more into the disgusting substance that is now my life, a body falls one hundred feet, plummeting from the canopy to the floor and let's hope to the hell below it.

We wait out the second one for twenty minutes before the corporal finally lets us get up.

Then three stand over one.

Tails has his face deep in the thick of the muck. The depth of him, the way so little is visible of his back and shoulders and helmet means he's been sinking into it for some time. Since we all hit the deck at the first shots.

Nobody is going to say it right now, but this, this is why you bayonet a body rather than shooting it. Don't attract any more attention than you're already going to draw. Even snipers get caught napping sometimes, but not if you set the alarm for them.

It is now a V patrol formation, with Corporal Havlicek at the point and his two gunners behind on each flank. We maintain a brisker pace than at any other time today. And a silence deeper and darker than all the Pacific nights so far combined.

The two buddies remain strong and together, now in lockstep toward our camp. Zachary Klecko has got a champion demolition man known as Tails strapped over his shoulder in an unbreakable fireman's carry. Because we are American marines and these are our guns and this is our duty, we look straight ahead and press on ahead in the way proud soldiers press on always. It is raining. A rain that would by now have defeated Noah is washing over us. I will not look but I can smell clearly through everything and I smell the tears washing down my old friend's face as heavily as this or any rain.

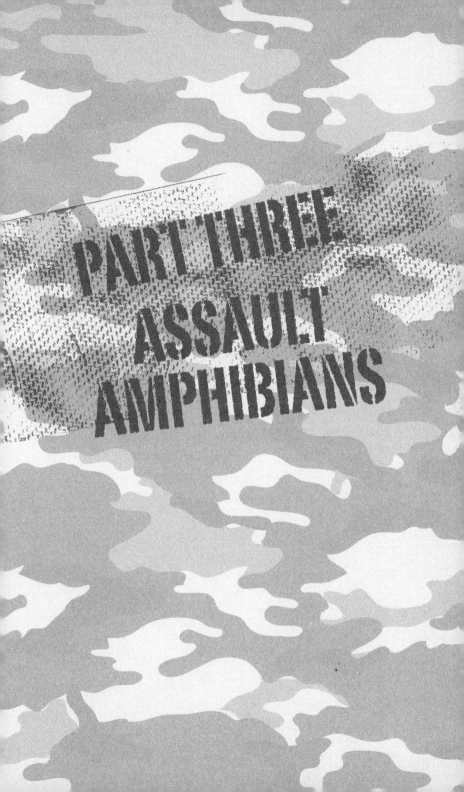

PART THREE

ASSAULT AMPHIBIANS

CHAPTER NINE

Hopping Islands

I'm pretty sure you killed him," I say to Klecko.

"Do you think so?"

"I do," I say, leaning in as if for a close inspection. "Yeah, I really do."

What I am not really inspecting is the very unfortunate and very dead man at the sharp end of my buddy's bayonet. Klecko is leaning into him with all his weight like Death's own farmer trying to turn over a stubborn chunk of turf.

It is also third-time unlucky for the guy, since various patrols have taken us past this same spot three times, and Zack thought he had a sneaky, suspicious look on his face each time.

I straighten up, concluding the inspection. He follows by slowly drawing the blade up and out of the corpse.

"You can't be too careful," he says, meaning it.

"No, you can't," I say. Because, you know, you really can't.

We knew that from the start, of course. But with every fresh start, new start, restart, stop-start, and jump start we know it a whole lot more.

We're on the island of Saipan, I think. They're all starting to blur — to *bleed together*, would be the most accurate way to put it. After Bougainville, everything accelerated, and new starts were indeed the order of the day, seemingly every day.

I suppose you'd say the biggest change was to our battalion, the Second Marine Parachute Battalion. That was changed a lot, because it was deactivated right out of business along with the rest of the Marine Parachute Regiment and all of the Marine Raiders. There now were no more "elite" specialist Marine operations teams because — as a lot of people believed from the beginning — *all* Marine divisions are elite.

So, the personnel all got assigned elsewhere, and a small number of companies, including the remains of our Company F from Bougainville, got shifted over to the Second Division. Different outfit, different job, different weapon, and, naturally, different island. There is no shortage of those from what I can tell.

And every one is the worst. Followed by the worst.

When we resume walking, once Klecko's guy is a certified kill for the third time, we walk through this cabbage patch of Japanese dead in search of one that needs to join them. It won't be far off, that much we know.

He's been different since Tails got killed, but I'm the only one who really knows. To the outside view and the guys working closely with him, if they see anything at all changed since then it's that he has become more serious, more focused, and more efficient. He does not make a wrong move or a decision that leaves anybody on our side at risk if he can eliminate that risk. These would be considered good changes, and they are, in military terms.

But I can see more. Any change from the Zachary Klecko that was already there would be unnecessary and not really welcome. We don't talk about it directly, but it is his turn to lean on me and I am there at every moment to make sure that he can.

"Don't you miss being a paramarine?" I ask him, just shooting the breeze, because it is a rare chance we have to shoot something so light and imaginary that even we can't shoot it to death. We are almost in a relaxed position, despite the fighting on Saipan being the highest pigpile of corpses of anything we have seen so far.

"Are you joking?" he says. "No. First, I love my gun now. The Browning Automatic Rifle wipes the floor with that stupid Reising that came out of a box of Cracker Jacks. And second, we never jumped, Nick."

"Yeah. The BAR is way better, fine. But I liked the idea, the identity, that came with being a para. I guess it's like how I feel when I get to tell people I play pro ball in the Red Sox organization. Even if it's only D-level so far, I got pride over that, same way. And, I would have liked to jump into combat at least once before they disbanded us."

"Yeah, uh-huh. Like all those Germans they dropped down on Crete. They got to jump once. Why not ask them how that was? Oh, that's right, we can't."

Troops on the ground in Crete were ready and waiting and shot those helpless paratroopers out of the sky while they floated to the ground. Like a murderous carnival game. I get an all-over shudder whenever it gets mentioned.

"Okay," I say. "I suppose that might have been a more horrible way to end the regiment than this was. But I'm never gonna dream about amphibious assaults the way I did about airborne drops behind enemy lines."

"Understood," he says, and resumes the meticulous care and cleaning and oiling of his beloved BAR.

Saipan's got a mountain range running steeply down the middle like a spine, and has surely and understandably had its back up the whole time we've been here. We're fighting north along the western slope of that spine toward the final objective, the airfield at Marpi Point on the very northern tip. We are nearly there, and have settled with most of our battalion into a shallow depression that's like an ice cream scoop out of the top of a hillock. It is our own islet of peaceful seclusion as night falls over an island that's still exploding and screaming everywhere else.

We are setting up to camp here for what should be the most normal and sane sleeping station of the whole campaign.

Then the peace is slaughtered as all at once there is a screaming, crazed, charging wild horde of Japanese soldiers coming up over the highest side of our comfortable bowl. That slope is the steepest, most heavily wooded, so our lookouts were few and probably inattentive and definitely dead.

All of our men rush into an old-style battle line and we open up an all-out barrage straight into the fearlessly crazy onslaught of the banzai charge.

Shoulder-to-shoulder-to-shoulder we stand and fire, and the killing is an unbelievable spectacle. Japanese fighters are dying, falling so fast in such great numbers that the ones behind are tripping over the ones hitting the ground in front of them. Then we kill them while they try to get up, while they keep on screaming until we shut them up with bullets. They try and shoot while they run but it is almost as if that isn't even the point, because their passion for running straight at us and our guns and death is the point of it all. And the screaming. The screaming, from fury, from agony, from hate, it is all in there and it looks like it could be an actual nightmare, an endless tidal wave of all the people we have killed along the way to this point coming back not to defeat us but to remind us.

On that score, if no other, they are successful. I am reminded, and sickened, and no matter how decisively we are winning this, I am absolutely terrified out of my wits.

When it is over I am numb, standing at my post with my furiously hot rifle smoking in my hands, observing a fresh harvest of mutilation covering our peaceful hilltop hideaway.

"Couldn't do that from a parachute, buddy," my buddy says.

Marpi Point is a perverse reverse of all that.

"No!" Klecko screams. "No, no, no, no, no!"

I am running along just behind him, toward the cliff edge high above the sea at Marpi. The battle for Saipan and its important airfields is won, and the Japanese feelings about no-surrender are now clearer than they have ever been. The commander, General Saito, and all his aides committed suicide three days ago. The mop-up of this island has been more literally exactly that than it was elsewhere, as we came to find more and more companies of dead soldiers who'd killed themselves rather than surrendering.

The Japanese garrison here had made use of thousands of native civilians on this island, and we saw too late the evidence of whole towns that had been wiped out by our artillery. When it was all coming apart toward the end, they started using the civilians for protection as we shot into cave after cave only to find that we had killed whole families to get to two noble soldiers cowering behind them.

How do we ever begin to make up for what is happening?

"No!" I echo my buddy as we make our final late lunge — and the whole crowd makes theirs.

The civilians who did not want to kill themselves are forced.

The dozen soldiers in uniform along the line yell

some long, passionate slogan in Japanese, and then they jump. The fifty or more women, children, and old folks all attached to the rope together jerk and buck as they are pulled, like the links of a bicycle chain, over the side.

"No, no, no, no" is all we can manage to scream. But I think we speak for everyone, everywhere, ever.

CHAPTER TEN

Easy

There's a magazine being circulated, and by the time I get my hands on it, it's softened and wrinkled as worn-out canvas, but the print is as clear as can be.

Brute Krulak is back in the States and he's becoming some kind of star representing the Marines in this war. One quote stands out, and as we try to relax as much as possible in the belly of our taxi, the latest amphibious landing craft to take us to the latest assault on the latest crucial island, I read it out loud to Klecko.

"'Japanese are really very easy to kill, because of the banzai charges. A man who goes directly into machine-gun fire generally loses his social security.'"

"Ha," Klecko says.

"Can you believe he's saying stuff like that to a big magazine?"

"Well, Nick, technically he's not wrong, is he?"

I feel myself getting a little flushed. "Well, Zack, I

suppose technically he's not," I say in less than my friendliest tone. I'm not even certain who I'm angry at.

"Are you all right?" he says, with a sudden sharp look of concern on his face.

"What? Why?"

"I think Nicky look sicky, that's why."

"Oh," I say, and now even that's making me angry. I stand up and head for the top deck to breathe and be by myself. "Choppy waters, is all. Getting a little seasick. Air. I need air, then I'll be right as rain."

How does anybody know whether he has a fever or not in these islands? Who can tell? This whole situation is a fever, is the truth of the matter. There are only two possibilities: you're either overheated, or you're dead.

"How are you holding up?" Corporal Havlicek asks as he reaches down and gives me a hand up out of my foxhole. The remains of our squad stayed together after we were shipped from one division to another. Four riflemen are also with us but I don't know them and have no intention of getting to know them. Or anybody else new, for that matter. Not before this thing is over. Un-knowing people is something I can live without now.

"I'm good, corporal, thanks. Sleeping better, for one."

In what has become the routine, I turn and give my partner a helping hand up from the hole. He gets halfway up before I lose my grip and he slides back down. I reach again and with some effort I get it right this time.

"Don't look at me like that," I say to Klecko. "It's not like you're a flyweight or nothing. Pulling the load of you up ain't easy."

He runs his hands up and down his sides, feeling his ribs. "It's forty pounds easier than it was two months ago," he says.

Everybody loses weight here. The food is not enough and everything else is way too much.

Havlicek grunts. "You have to tell me if anything is really wrong, okay?" His stare, straight into my eyes and trying to look beyond, is both really nice and really uncomfortable.

"Of course, corporal," I say, and he nods politely and takes his dubious expression to go check on the next guys.

And of course I won't tell him, and of course lots of things are wrong. The fever, the rash everywhere, the headache that is my new best friend. I am weak, and want to throw up all the time; I bruise too easily and sometimes I bleed when there isn't even a cut. Blood just sort of rises to the surface of my skin and exits the wreckage of me.

But everybody here has all that, so what business have I got to go bellyaching about my bellyache? This will all be over soon, and everybody can get right then.

Nobody's going anywhere without me.

My buddy points at my face. "Got a little nosebleed there, buddy," he says, looking far more panicked about it than I would think necessary.

I laugh and wipe it with the back of my hand, which looks like it's bleeding most of the time anyway.

"You sure you're okay?" he says.

"I am okay, Zack. But I have to admit Tinian is tough. This is the worst one yet, don't you agree?"

This worries his face more than the blood did.

"I probably would agree, Nicky. If we were still on Tinian. We left there five weeks ago. This is Peleliu."

This information does not help me at all. I feel panicky, and can feel the desperation sweat rolling down my face. I get light-headed.

"Yeah, I know. Of course I know where we are. I was just saying that Tinian was the worst so far, even worse than Peleliu, so maybe that's a turning point and things are looking up finally."

He nods, nods some more, and then, unfortunately, speaks.

"Nothing in human history was worse than Peleliu. Did Tinian have the cannibals, Nicky? You remember the cannibals, of course. The captured marines we found carved into chops and steaks and cutlets? The fake surrenders? Do you remember how we lost Bryant and Westphal? The *surrenders* who had explosives taped all around their waists? Sure you do. We took Peleliu all right, but we gave those guys and a lot more in the trade."

"Zack, stop it. I'm not quitting."

"I know what you'll remember. Remember when we landed on Saipan, after the first slugfest for the beach? When we moved our way up inland and . . ."

". . . baseball fields," I say, seeing them clearly now.

"Baseball fields, right. How could baseball fields be here? How could the game be here? How could people who played baseball, people who went to the trouble . . ."

"And they were not bad fields . . ."

"They were not, that's right. Remember how they made you feel, Nick? Remember how you —"

"I did not cry. You made that up."

"Okay, anyway, we were there, all that time, together. And I was leaning hard on you then, because I needed to. That's what buddies do."

"It's what they do."

"What the buddy system is for."

"Yeah, it is. But we got through, and now we are here."

"Here, yes. Remember the landing here, how much fun we had? Remember the tank crews caught on the coral, sitting ducks, then drowning right there in the tanks as they went under? Remember getting to the beach, so many dead marines and the land crabs already eating the bodies, swarming all over them, those land crabs . . ."

I cannot fight the nausea if he doesn't stop.

"Stop, Zack. Stop it. We said we would be inseparable, and we will not separate. *Never to sever.* You told me nobody would ever separate us — including me."

He does not debate any specific point. He probably knows he doesn't have to.

"It's my turn," he says quietly. "You've been carrying me since Tails. Don't you think I know that? We have killed people in caves by every method available to us, short of the flamethrower, so I think you've accomplished everything you can."

I remember now. God, I remember and I am remembering every single one as they file past me like a newsreel of my own personal horrors. Throwing grenades into caves and tunnels when we didn't know who was down there. Blasting them with gunfire because no one would answer when we gave them the chance and they didn't take it. The locals, the families weren't even Japanese. Of course they didn't answer; they thought we were as bad as the other guys were. But we weren't. Until, then we were.

I think I want to talk, think I want to answer, think briefly that I can do it, but in the end I am just shaking my head at him, just shaking no, no, no.

And just in time, naturally just in time, Zachary Klecko reaches out and grabs me as I fall, collapsing forward. I plant my face in his hard chest rather than into the dirt I was headed for. He holds me tight and supports me because my legs are doing no such thing. And because maybe it is his turn.

CHAPTER ELEVEN

Severed

The next time I open my eyes, I'm in a hospital, and Klecko is on Iwo Jima.

"Excuse me, please?" I say to one of the many nurses sprinting from patient to patient.

"Yes, hi," she says. "Sorry, I don't mean to neglect you. But as you can see, there are cases here that are a lot more urgent than yours."

"But I can't see anything but a lot of chaos and running around," I say. "That's the thing. Can you tell me how I got here, when I got here, why I'm even here? Did I lose my legs?"

She scowls down at me. A military nurse is probably the only person in the world who can get angry at somebody who asks that question.

"No," she says. "Why even ask me that?"

I point to the corner, to what looks like a laundry bin. Except for all the bloody arms and legs protruding up out of it. Like a desperate rabble is down beneath begging for help.

The nurse barks, like maybe she's the boss, "Can someone please remove the limb basket? I did ask for somebody to take care of this before. Honestly."

A more junior-looking nurse rushes up and shoves the basket away while I could swear a few of the hands wave me good-bye.

"Okay," the nurse says. "First, I hope it will be a bonus now, to know that you still have legs. Unfortunately you also have dengue fever, malaria, and the early stages of some jungle rot that will look more hideous than it actually is, so try not to look at your feet and ankles for a while."

"Fine," I say, "the thing is, when do I go back and link up with my squad?"

She looks at me in the sad way a healthy person in a hospital bed doesn't wish to be looked at. "Ah, darlin', just sit still and the doctor will talk to you about that."

I sit still, and eventually the doctor talks to me about that.

CHAPTER TWELVE

April Fools

I spend six weeks in the hospital before being released. Around the same time, my guys spend almost as much time on Iwo Jima before being released.

I feel so much stronger than when I fell into my buddy's arms on Peleliu. I feel rebuilt by the incredible medical folks, and recharged over the fact that I'm going back to my team.

We reunite in time to board a Landing Vehicle, Tracked (LVT), affectionately called The Water Buffalo. It's April Fools' Day, 1945.

"Corporal Havlicek!" I shout when I see him. He comes straight over and gives me a strong, lean hug. He's never done that before.

"Didn't expect to ever see you again," he says. "Not after what you looked like."

"Just needed some rest," I say. "That's all it was. Doctors said I must have been brutally overworked by the non-coms running my squad."

"Yes, I'm sure that's what they said," he says, laughing. "I am famously responsible for more of the carnage winding up at the hospital than any bombs, bullets, or bugs. I'm sure they'll eventually send me a bill. The important thing is, you are fit and back in the fight."

"Yes, sir, rested and ready. We're back together now, gonna take Okinawa, and pray that the Japanese see some sense before we have to go knocking on doors on the mainland. Where are the other guys?"

He nods, tips his head at a sideways sympathy angle.

"There have been a lot of challenges, Nick."

Havlicek never once came close to calling me by my first name before. I thought I would like it. Right now it gives me the chills.

"Been challenges every step of the way, corporal. So, where are the guys?"

"They're on Iwo Jima," the voice says right into my ear.

I jump with the fright. When I turn to see that the voice belongs to Zachary Klecko, I also see that his face has changed, again, or more, but he is a different guy from the one I got separated from.

I pretty nearly launch myself as a human rocket, to hug him.

He feels a little stiff, but not too bad.

"I sorta missed having you around, Nardini," he says. "Seems like they took good care of you, though."

"They did. I'm good. I wish I could have been there on Iwo to help you guys, though, Zack. I should have been there with you."

He holds up a hand. "No. You were weakened to the point of uselessness by the diseases. You'd have been less than no help if I had to hump up and down Iwo with you strapped to my back the whole time. Not that I wouldn't have done it, though. Anyway, I didn't really need any help."

I laugh, for the first time in a while.

"Cleaned up the whole island by yourself, did you, Zachary?"

"Not quite all by myself," he says grimly.

"We're the only ones who came back, Nick," Havlicek says solemnly. "We are the demolished demolition squad. Silas was the last."

"He was a good man," I say.

"He was," Havlicek says. "And for a sergeant, that may well have been a first."

I laugh, but not like I can feel it. I look back to my buddy. I never should have let anybody separate us.

"Zack?" I ask tentatively.

"Zeke," he says.

"What?"

"Zeke. Call me that. The guys, the new guys in the battalion, they eventually worked out my initials, started playing with them, and eventually I was Zeke. ZK, right? Zeke? Well they gave me that name and I'm Zeke now. So call me Zeke, and not any of that old stuff, right? From now on. Right?"

I look hard at him for the gag. Nothing.

"Right," I say. "Of course, Zeke, absolutely, whatever you want, buddy."

"Now," he says, putting up his hands for me and Havlicek to grasp, "let's go finish off little ol' Okinawa and finally get to the real business of invading that Japanese mainland, huh?"

We all clasp hands and bear down on Okinawa ahead, and the end of resistance once and for all.

"I'm doing this here for friendship," Havlicek says, squeezing and waving our hands back and forth above us. "And for respect. But Nick, I can assure you that after Iwo Jima, your buddy here is the *only* person looking forward to fighting the Japanese on their home island."

Klecko coughs out a bark of a laugh and throws down our hands. "I didn't say I was looking forward to it . . . and I'm sure I'm not the only one, anyway."

"Let's just fight Okinawa like we never want to fight again, then," I say.

"Let's," Havlicek says, and turns away to talk to another corporal who's clapped his shoulder.

"Oh, and guess what?" Klecko says when we're alone on a crowded Water Buffalo. He sniffs me in an obvious way that accuses me of being hospital clean.

"What's that, Zack?"

"Zeke, I told you. I'm Zeke, remember?"

"Sorry, Zeke. So, what?"

"I finally got to use a flamethrower. A *lot*. You missed it, but that's okay. It was incredible. I'm now the number one expert chef in the field of Japanese barbecue."

I stare at him with his unfamiliar and strained smile. The smile-like thing I offer in return feels just as unnatural.

Zeke wants me to hear his boasting and give him a shocked reaction.

Zack wants me to hear something else, and give him something better.

We can do better. I don't have the right words, but I hope my slow, sustained nodding tells him we can do better, we will do better.

———————— ★ ————————

The slaughter rule.

"Why don't they just quit?" I scream to be heard by my friend as we again pour round after round after round into a bunker built into the side of a small, bald hill in the middle of this sad, sandblasted landscape.

We stop to reload and listen for anything. The smoke from the guns is the only bearable smell and it lasts only an instant.

There is no new noise from the bunker. Since we've been assaulting it for nearly an unbroken hour, no noise is good noise.

"They should have the slaughter rule like in baseball, where if the score is thirty to nothing after three innings they just call the game over."

"If they did that," Klecko says, "they would have called the game over when they saw us sailing into the harbor."

He's right about that. The fleet assembled for this assault totaled over thirteen hundred warships. I remember looking back briefly from the beachhead and thinking we had so many ships in this thing they could supply us just by lining up from here to San Diego and passing everything along hand to hand to hand.

The shelling of the island in advance of our landings has left an already barren volcanic rock almost a moonscape. Most buildings and vegetation are already laid waste before we go to work on them.

The effect is like if you took one of the early overgrown, overgreen islands — Bougainville, maybe — and skinned it like a rabbit, the way a guy pulls the pelt up and over the animal's head and leaves it inside out. Like we just reached right down the island's throat and pulled it inside out and what we got was Okinawa.

We land over a half million troops, which is more than triple the population of the island in peacetime.

Peacetime. What a thought.

But none of that is enough to convince these fighters to give up. Nothing is enough.

CHAPTER THIRTEEN

Liberation

Our swift and satisfying victory on Okinawa takes three months. It costs 50,000 Americans killed or wounded and 100,000 Japanese, and satisfies nobody, really.

We are at Camp Tarawa in Hawaii, preparing for the unthinkable invasion of mainland Japan, while US aircraft set city after city there alight with incendiary bombing raids that *still* don't persuade the enemy to surrender. That willingness to dig in and die has us all second-guessing. Even my tireless buddy has had his head turned.

We're enjoying comfort and civilization like we haven't known for some time, headed from our dry bunks to eat our hot breakfasts when he says, "If they were willing to defend a couple of nothing rocks like Iwo and Oki as if they were saving their own mothers from the lions, what will they do on home soil?"

"You're saying what every man here is thinking, pal," I say.

We're still thinking it, staring into our eggs, when the announcement comes over the loudspeaker that an American B-29 Superfortress has dropped the largest bomb ever seen, on the city of Hiroshima.

We are eating again three days later when the system blares out news of the second atomic bombing, on the city of Nagasaki.

Two bombs, and that's what did it.

Turns out both missions were launched from the airstrip at Tinian.

"So, we did our part when we secured the island for the airstrip," Klecko says, eating a lot more robustly this time. "That's what all that fuss was for to take that nasty, grubby little place."

"I guess so," I say, suddenly unable to eat anything at all. I put my utensils down on my tin plate, sit back in my seat, and rest my hands in my lap. "Then what about all the nasty, grubby places we took since then, a whole year's worth of fighting? Was it even necessary? Maybe we could have stopped at Saipan and Tinian, and got the same result we have now?"

There is a clear and distinct message in my friend's refusal to look up, in his aggressive scraping of a tin plate that has no food left on it. "Can't we just be glad it's over, Nicky?"

You would think so, wouldn't you?

As it happens, we do make it to the Japanese mainland. We are part of the occupation force, assigned to one of the POW recovery teams tasked with liberating the prisoners from the camps and getting them back on the road home.

I look forward to this job, which promises to be the first truly positive and rewarding assignment in memory.

However, ten minutes after walking through the gates leading into Kamioka Branch Camp, all I want to do is walk back out again.

"We killed guys who still looked better than this," Klecko observes as we round up hundreds of former fighting men wearing nothing but shorts or strips of white sheet fashioned into something diaper-like. Their heads look, to a man, like oversize doll's heads wedged onto bodies that couldn't possibly support them. The ribs visible all around us look sharp enough to cut our hands if we touch them, which I am not anxious to do.

"Hang in there, buddy," Zachary Klecko, my Zachary Klecko, says when he figures me out. "These boys need us, and they're gonna get us, right?"

"Right," I say, and take the hand of one wobbly bone rack who is too weak to make it up the ramp onto the transport truck. He stalls, and I escort him. As I ease him into his seat, I have a hand around his rib cage. Feels like I could close my hand completely around it.

I pass Klecko helping the next man as I walk back down the ramp to fetch another one. This one isn't even trying. I cannot see his face because his head is slumped, but I can see his torso and arms covered in open sores, lacerations, and bruises from beatings.

Kamioka was a forced labor camp. This guy apparently required a lot of forcing, right till the end.

"Come with me, sir," I say, grabbing both of his hands.

He looks up and into my eyes from a spot six thousand miles away.

"Have you seen Theo?" he asks in a rasp. "Have you talked to my brother, Theo? Is he all right?"

I can't believe I'm seeing and hearing this. It could be, must be, a hallucination.

"Do you know who I am?" I say, because his eyes will not confirm anything.

He doesn't hesitate for an instant.

"You're the loudmouth clown who plays left field for the Centreville Red Sox," he says.

In yet another in a long line of insane, upside-down moments from this long, awful war, this frail and broken man remains unemotional while his rescuer can hardly speak. I am sobbing so hard I can just about ask, "Are you Hank McCallum?"

"I am Hank McCallum," he says flatly. "My brother is Theo McCallum, Army Air Corps. Have you spoken to him? Do you know where he is?"

I shake my head no, his eyes roll down, and his knees buckle.

I catch Hank McCallum, and I pick him up in my arms. I walk up the ramp carrying him like a child into the truck. It is so easy to do this, no effort required at all.

"We'll find your brother, Hank. We'll find him. We'll all go home now. Let's go home and play some ball."

Zack never met Hank, but on the way down the ramp he pats his head lightly, saying, "Yeah, boys. Let's all go home and play some ball."

Yeah. Let's.

About the Author

Chris Lynch is the author of numerous acclaimed books for middle-grade and teen readers, including the Vietnam series and the National Book Award finalist *Inexcusable*. He teaches in the Lesley University creative writing MFA program and divides his time between Massachusetts and Scotland.

DATE			